Some days you walk into a trap filled with surprises.

Nick's heart beat hard in his chest and his grip on the butt of his blaster tightened as the echo of multiple footsteps filled the tunnel. The sounds were coming from the direction they'd just come from.

Abruptly the footsteps ceased. Nick strained to hear any sounds but heard nothing.

"Place your weapons on the ground," said a high-pitched voice that could be female. He never made assumptions based on such limited information, so the speaker could be male for all he knew.

"No. We're here to rescue our friend. Once we see her, we will surrender our weapons," Nick said over the external speaker of his suit. There was a pause, then he thought he heard a whispered argument. Finally the voice spoke again. "Is your friend Sirenna Albright?"

Nick froze, sucking in a breath. *What is happening? Does everyone on this planet know Siren?* "Yes. Do you know where she is?"

"If you lower your weapons, we will talk." Talking was Nick's preferred method of communication. Shooting didn't resolve much of anything and it could make you very dead, very quickly. "Why should we trust you?"

"Because I am her sister, Sonara Albright."

Blaster Squad #3

Planet of Doom

By

Russ Crossley

Published by 53rd Street Publishing

Offices in Gibsons, B.C. Canada and Lincoln City

Oregon, U.S.A

Blaster Squad Series

#1 Terror on the Moon

#2 Sea of Death

#3 Planet of Doom

#4 Raiders of Cloud City (coming soon)

Acknowledgments

Thank you to, Kris and Dean for the confidence and inspiration in those early days of my writing career.

Dedication

For the fans of science fiction who inspire me every day to write these stories.

Blaster Squad #3
Planet of Doom

Published by 53rd Street Publishing

Copyright © 2016 Russ Crossley
All rights reserved

Cover art © Can Stock Photo Inc. / helenfield

Cover designed by R. Edgewood
Cover design and layout © 2016 by 53rd Street
Publishing
Print ISBN 978-1927-6215-16

53rd Street Publishing
Head office: Gibsons B.C. Canada
www.53rdstreetpublishing.com

Introduction

The series is progressing as I envisioned it would. The danger and excitement still feels fresh and I'm having a great time writing about these characters. They surprise me as much as I'm sure the readers are.

Thank you for the continuing support of the fans, and my team at 53rd Street Publishing for their support in the telling of these stories.

See you all on our next trip to the far future.

Russ Crossley
Gibsons, B.C.
May 2016

1

Navy Officers' Quarters
Alliance Station
Orbiting Earth's moon
4125.9.15 Galactic

SIRENNA ALBRIGHT STOPPED moving and held her breath. Her senses were on high alert.

Listening intently, Sirenna strained to detect any sound in the still air of her quarters. Someone or something had moved, penetrating her consciousness as she finished peeling off her training gear in preparation for a muscle-soothing shower. The salty perspiration bathing the naked skin of her lithe, athletic frame filled her nostrils as her olfactory senses sniffed for a scent that shouldn't be here.

A tingle of peppermint tickled her nostrils, making her stomach muscles tense and a knot of tension form in the pit of her stomach. She detested peppermint in all its forms.

Her yellow, almond-shaped eyes flitted to the discarded gun belt that lay around her bare feet where her blaster was still in its holster, her razor-sharp fighting knife and baton were in their separate compartments ready for deployment. Only this time, whoever had infiltrated her quarters had caught her with her pants down. *Literally*, she thought with grim amusement.

Sirenna prepared for unarmed combat by sliding her left foot backward slowly until it was behind her, in line with her shoulders, which were turned slightly. She then shifted her right foot to a sideways position in relation to her body to add to her stability. She extended her left arm, pushing it straight out, forty-five degrees from her body, her hand forming a fist while pulling her right arm back forming an L-shape, tight against her right torso, waist high, her palm up, fingers curling into a tight second fist.

Her six-foot-tall, hundred and sixty pounds of muscle and sinew were now perfectly balanced and ready to repel an attack. Not an attack from a blaster, obviously, but she would make any attacker pay dearly.

Her eyes widened with surprise when a shadowy figure wearing dull purple blast armor suddenly appeared, standing to her right no more than two feet away. Without hesitation, Sirenna stepped back and to her left, swinging her shoulders square to her target. She shot her right arm out to block the attacker's blast rifle that was swinging toward her. Her blow was strong enough and placed at just the right spot along the length of barrel that it snapped into two pieces.

This didn't slow the attacker, who dropped the now useless weapon, the pieces clattering across the floor, and pulled a long-bladed knife from a sheath attached to the belt around its waist.

Sirenna now had her body square to the attacker. She slapped the palms of her hands on the sides of the cool steel blade and twisted. This caused the attacker to lose its grip of the weapon. Sirenna now had control of the thick-handled, eight-inch-long knife.

Before the attacker could react a second time, Sirenna flipped the knife over, catching it in midair, then, with all her strength, slipped it between the gaps in the attacker's armor. The gaps were necessary to allow the wearer flexibility to move their arms and legs during combat. A fine, strong, plasti-steel mesh protected these vulnerable junctions between the armor plates.

But Sirenna knew that, with sufficient force, she could pierce the mesh and slip the sharp blade into the flesh beyond. Especially when her attacker was within striking distance.

Sirenna grunted as the knife sank up to the hilt.

The attacker froze, then sagged to its knees until it collapsed to the floor like a balloon with a leak, landing in a heap on its right side. Blood seeped from the wound, pooling around the body. The attacker grunted in pain and shock. Sirenna couldn't see its face behind the helmet covering its features, but the chest moved up and down, meaning it was alive.

Sirenna grunted her distain, a sardonic grin spreading across her face.

She squatted next to the armored attacker and checked the belt for other weapons. Seeing none, she grasped the knife's handle and extracted it from the tear in the mesh. Blood the color of purple grape juice coated the blade.

She studied the helmet and managed to locate the clasp that would unlatch it. She did so and pulled it off the head.

Black eyes a deep shade of obsidian were dulled by pain, and purple blood trickled from the right side of the wide mouth. She was unable to determine the gender by the appearance alone.

"Who are you?" asked Sirenna.

"I…bounty…" the attacker gasped, then stiffened, and the grayish purple flesh of its angular face lost what little color remained. The light in the eyes faded until the body sagged when the last of its strength ebbed and was gone. Air escaped the lungs for the last time. The voice sounded female. Regardless, he or she was dead. *Bounty hunter?*

Sirenna studied the face as a slow frown creased her forehead. After removing the helmet completely, revealing short hair the color of golden, sun-washed wheat, the frown deepened even more. *Something isn't right.*

Sirenna reached to her own gun belt still on the floor and extracted her baton after setting the attacker's knife on the floor. Using the baton, she turned the attacker's head to the right and looked at the flesh where the neck met the beginning of the jawline. Her eyes drifted to the neck. No Adam's apple. She sucked in a little air and her eyes widened briefly. The bounty hunter definitely wasn't male, and she wasn't an alien.

This dead bounty hunter was a human female, surgically altered to appear alien. Sirenna assumed the blood had also been chemically changed to appear non-human.

Who would go to such trouble? And why did they want her dead?

Sirenna wondered if this bounty hunter had something to do with Nick Justice's offer of a job with the mercenary team he was forming called Blaster Squad. If that were true, then Blaster Squad would be a highly dangerous, high action-oriented job unlike anything she'd ever enjoyed in the Alliance Navy as a self-defense training contractor.

"Sounds like fun," she murmured.

2

SEVERAL WEEKS AFTER arriving at Armstrong shipyards, the GSS *Hunter* was finally able to maneuver under its own power. Gears piloted the ship from his usual seat in the pilot's seat, scanning the horseshoe shape created by the five screens feeding him information about the ship's systems. His ocular implants whirred in the quiet of the flight deck as they shifted in and out to enhance his view of various quadrants of the screens.

Beside the pilot, Nick sat in the copilot's seat, sipping coffee from a mug he'd brought with him from the galley. He'd fully recovered from his wounds incurred on their last mission. Gears had wanted to make this routine test run solo but Nick insisted on coming along. There was never anything he would describe as routine when it involved Blaster Squad. "What do you think, Gears?"

"Hmmm…well, Captain, the repairs are okay but the new attitude flight propulsion jets are not the best. They react sluggishly." He snorted derisively. "You know what engineers are like, they always have to improve things. But improvements are not always the way to go, especially because they so often forget to ask the end users what they need or want."

Suddenly his voice became tense. "Sir, sensors report there is a ship five thousand kilometers off our port side that's going to intersect our projected flight path."

Nick took a sip of the warm, milky coffee and swallowed. He wasn't concerned.

With all the surveillance drones and automated warning buoys scattered around Earth's solar system, the odds of a collision with another vessel were so low as to be microscopic. Regardless, Gears would avoid any contact with the other ship.

"I'll check their transponder," he said in a sleepy voice. He was going to retire to his quarters soon for a short nap before Gears returned them to the shipyard. The brilliant tech genius would no doubt have extensive notes for the repair engineers and he didn't want to be regaled with all the technical details. *All I need is a tall ship and a sea to sail her in*, he mused.

Nick hadn't bothered to turn on any of the screens at the copilot's workstation before leaving the shipyard, so he first had to turn them on by pressing the flat red button on the console. The four screens flickered to life. He lifted his mug to his lips to take another sip as the transponder information of the approaching vessel appeared as a list on the screen to his right.

He swallowed before speaking. "It's a spice trader from Takdon III. According to its flight plan, they're carrying a load of white, red, and black pepper destined for the Asian Commonwealth on Earth."

"Okay, boss, if you say so, but why are they charging six blaster cannon batteries on their hull and increasing speed?"

Nick coughed and his heart rate increased. "Impossible. Spice traders carry minimal weapons."

"I suspect, sir, *this* spice trader is not a spice trader."

"Gears, evasive maneuvers. Set course back to the shipyard." Nick hadn't bothered to put on his seat straps since this was to be a short systems test flight, not a firefight. He slipped the seat belt straps over his shoulders, clipped the ends into the slots at his sides, then pulled the straps snug. "I'll signal the navy to request backup."

He was glad he'd gotten the straps secured when the *Hunter* began to shimmy as Gears made an aggressive course change, firing the steering rockets along the left side of the ship's hull simultaneously. G forces pressed Nick hard against the left side of the seat and a change in gravity made his stomach heave. He threw his mug to the deck, where it bounced, shooting his remaining coffee into the air, then fell on its side and skittered away until it struck a bulkhead and stopped.

Nick opened the emergency naval channel by pressing a digital button along the bottom of the screen to his left. He had to hold his breath and force his fingers to move to the left, but he managed to reach and press the button anyway. "GSS *Hunter* to Alliance Navy. We are under attack by unknown intruder disguising their transponder as a spice trader. Requesting immediate assistance."

Silence. Nick tried again with the same result. He sucked in some air and his stomach muscles tightened. They had just fixed the *Hunter* and he'd be dammed if some unknown ship was going to blow it apart.

"Gears," he said between gritted teeth. "Ready on weapons and shields?"

"Of course, sir," replied Gears, an edge of unrestrained glee in his tone.

Nick smiled to himself. Whoever was trying to stop them had someone on the inside. The sudden appearance of this warship confirmed what he had suspected.

Back at the shipyard after Gears told him the weapons and shields were repaired on the *Hunter,* Nick had instructed the tech genius to omit the repairs from his daily progress report to the yardmaster. Evidently, whoever was behind this attack had access to those reports.

When Gears filed the flight plan for the systems flight test, Nick had thought the traitor might see an opportunity to put the *Hunter*, and them, out of action permanently.

"Are the new shields as good as you said they are?" Gears nodded. "And the weapons?"

Gears glanced to his side at Nick in the copilot's seat. "Better. Sir."

Nick offered his friend a sardonic grin. "Well, then, whoever this is is gonna get more than they bargained for."

3

GEARS FIRED THE main battery as soon as the attacking vessel came within range.

The enemy ship's shields glowed on Nick's right side screen, then it shot away, the sublight engines having engaged when the wave of blaster energy contacted their shields.

Curious, thought Nick. "Gears, can we keep up with them?"

"No problem, Captain."

Nick had rerouted the sensor reports from the sensor officer's station to the screen to his left in the copilot's workstation. He studied the sensor readings until they were once again within blaster cannon range of the enemy vessel. "Gears, hold your fire," he instructed the tech genius.

"But, sir, we can disable them."

Nick glanced at Gears. "Yes, we can, but it wouldn't be a fair fight."

Gears looked at Nick, surprise registering on his face. "Five of those blaster cannon batteries are inoperable. The one that is operational is low powered. It's doubtful if the lone cannon is capable of penetrating our shields. The only way it would affect us is if we had no defensive screens at all."

"That doesn't make sense, Captain," said Gears, shaking his bald head. "They are using an attack vector common to navy vessels on a collision run. They may not be able to penetrate our shields, but they are certainly going to try and take us out. It's suicide, sir."

Nick grimaced. Gears was right, it was suicide. But why? "When they pass within range, I want you to punch a hole in their shields and disable their engines. Then I want you to open a visual communication channel with their flight deck." His eyes narrowed. "I need a heart-to-heart with whoever's in charge."

"Aye, sir," said Gears, turning his attention back to the control systems on his console.

Nick watched the enemy vessel begin its run on the expected attack vector just as Gears said they would. *At least some things are universal.* When the enemy ship was within a thousand meters of the *Hunter*'s position,

Blaster Squad #3 Planet of Doom

Gears fired a narrow beam of blaster energy at a spot on the enemy hull where the engines were. There was a brief glow, then the vessel shuddered and its momentum slowed. The speed achieved would remain constant but they would be unable to make any further course adjustments without an operational engine.

"Channel open," said Gears softly. He understood lives aboard that vessel were at stake and whoever they were had taken a great risk by making such a reckless attack.

Nick's center screen flickered once, then steadied, showing the image of a ship's bridge of a type he had never seen before. Also in the image was a helmeted figure covered in purplish battle armor. The helmet's visor obscured the wearer's face.

"This is Nick Justice of Blaster Squad. Whom am I addressing?"

"Sub-Protector Lal speaking." The alien's voice sounded odd, not male or female, though it spoke Galactic English with a Martian accent, reminiscent of Russian mingled with Italian. *I've heard this accent somewhere before.* It suddenly dawned on him; Bones had the same accent. Could this alien be a Martian?

"Why are you attacking us, Sub-Protector?"

14

The alien was silent for several seconds, then said, "Sirenna Albright killed my mate."

Nick considered the alien's revelation and searched his memory for any recollection about Siren's past that involved the death of an alien woman fitting the general description of this male. When she joined the squad, she told him of the attack in her quarters at Alliance Station in 4125. His eyes narrowed. "Your mate attempted to murder my second in command. She defended herself." He paused to allow the alien to respond. When he didn't say anything, Nick added, "She expressed her regrets to me for your mate's death, but Siren had no idea her attacker had a mate."

The alien responded immediately this time. "If this is true, then she should be willing to surrender to me for judgment."

Without realizing it, Nick had painted himself into a corner. *How am I supposed to get Siren out of this one?* "Why don't we take your dispute to a representative of the Alliance Council and let them decide if she should be turned over to you?"

"We are *not* members of the Alliance," the alien said curtly.

"Yes, I know, but the Alliance could act as an impartial arbitrator.

They have more than a thousand years' experience in galactic law and negotiations." Nick really hoped the alien agreed to his suggestion. Otherwise he'd have to start firing, and the last thing Nick wanted was to start a shooting war with an alien race. These guys didn't seem to accept no for an answer, so even if he destroyed their ship, no doubt others would follow, and they'd no doubt shoot first and ask questions afterward.

"Yes," the alien finally replied. "I agree to meet with an Alliance Council representative."

A wave of relief relaxed the tension that had formed between Nick's shoulder blades. The issue now was who on the council would agree to meet with this alien to discuss Siren's extradition? Blaster Squad had enemies on the council who would love to see them hauled off to some kangaroo court on an alien world. Whoever it was he hoped they did what was right. Nick would accept nothing less.

4

Alliance Command Headquarters
Alliance Station
Orbiting Earth's moon
4146.8.3 Galactic

NICK STOOD BESIDE Sub-Protector Lal, waiting for Alliance Council Chairman Edgar Whizzar to appear from the private lift behind his expansive plasti-steel desk. To their left was a wall of floor to ceiling windows through which the gray surface of Earth's moon slowly moved under them. The ashen surface was dotted with nests of light as they passed over the domed cities that dotted the landscape of the dead moon.

Al-Mok Talon, Head of Alliance Security Services, sat silently in a low-back chair, his legs crossed, his brilliant green eyes watchful. On the right side of his hip hung a faux-leather holster. Nick saw the large butt of a blaster pistol. He didn't recognize the design.

From the look of distain on his narrow, rust-colored features,

Nick suspected Talon preferred to shoot first, never intending to ask any questions before or after. But until the chairman had a chance to talk with them first, Talon would wait for the order to strike. Talon was well aware of which side of his *pelak* bread was slathered in *klut* oil.

Nick had to stop himself from gagging at the thought of the dry-as-dust *pelak* bread swathed with the rotten-fish smelling oil. *Etes eat god-awful crap.*

He smirked in Talon's direction before turning his attention to the lift doors cycling open. Whizzar stepped out, accompanied by his aide, Mili Pumpel, a human born on the Surveyor Habitat orbiting Mars. She grew up in the Mars Prime Corporation Dome until she joined the company as one of Whizzar's many executive vice presidents.

Mili bled corporate blood from her pores; her loyalty was absolute. Her tanned features were marred by a deep scowl wrinkling her forehead when she saw Nick waiting for them. He noted she wore her hair in a tight bun atop her oblong-shaped head. Her makeup was flawlessly applied, not too pretty, but attractive in the right light. She wore an expensive looking gray pantsuit and designer green-and-white striped shirt under the suit jacket.

Mili and Nick had dated for a short few weeks five years ago. The brief fling ended badly. Evidently she hadn't forgotten him or the nature of their disagreement. Nick certainly hadn't.

As Whizzar's Executive Vice President of Corporate Relations, Mili Pumpel knew of the meeting but she probably hoped some intruder had vaporized him on the way here.

Nick offered her a humorless smile, which Mili ignored on her way to sit in the chair set against the wall behind Whizzar's desk to his right. She was quite literally the chairman's right hand.

Mili's attention was focused on her handheld unit that was capable of functioning as everything from scheduler to comm unit to galactic web browser to projection device for online meetings to the weather service reporting for every world in the Alliance. It stored trillions of pictures and recorded countless hours of digital images. It also acted as a translation device capable of understanding the languages of every Alliance world, and Nick assumed some languages outside Alliance controlled space.

Nick often said he'd never own one of those comm thingamajigs unless they could make a decent cup of coffee.

So far, the tech types had been unable to meet his requirements, not even Gears, though he had tried and failed several times over the years.

When he and Mili were a couple, Nick learned she had majored at university in cultural diversity, eventually achieving a double PhD on the subject. She would have made a skilled diplomat but chose the private sector because they paid better.

No kidding, he thought, eyeing her expensive clothes and shoes.

Whizzar sat in his executive chair behind the desk and motioned for Nick and Sub-Protector Lal to take seats opposite him in the two chairs provided for this purpose.

Nick glanced at Lal, who had refused to remove his helmet at the security checkpoint when they entered the headquarters complex. This was when Talon had been contacted. Once Nick explained to the security head that Siren's extradition was in play and that only Whizzar could make the final decision, Talon reluctantly agreed to allow Lal to keep his helmet on.

Whizzar regarded them with skeptical eyes, alternating between Nick and Lal. His scowl seemed to deepen with each passing second of silence.

Nick had to bury the urge to start fidgeting as they waited.

Finally Whizzar said, "Sub-Protector, it is a pleasure to meet you. I understand you are seeking to extradite an Alliance citizen for an alleged crime you claim occurred more than twenty years ago." He paused to take in a breath. "In fact, a crime you say happened on this station."

Sub-Protector Lal sat silently for several seconds without responding. Nick began to wonder if the alien was still alive or was perhaps deaf and hadn't heard the chairman.

When he spoke, his deep voice startled Nick. "If you refuse to surrender Sirenna Albright to me, there will be serious consequences."

Whizzar's eyes narrowed and his features darkened. "Are you threatening the Alliance, Mr. Lal?" Nick noted Whizzar abandoned Lal's title for effect.

"I am only stating facts," said Lal confidently.

Nick noticed Lal had never referred to the chairman by either name or title. The sub-protector evidently recognized neither as worthy. *Lal is clearly focused on his goal.* This did not bode well for Siren.

His second in command hadn't taken the news well that Lal wanted to avenge the death of his mate all those years ago. Nick assured Siren she'd had no choice at the time. Since she had no idea her attacker had a mate, the fact Lal wanted her to pay for the death twenty-three years later seemed unusual, to say the least.

Why had Lal waited this long to seek justice for his mate's death? He evidently had a starship and could have made his claim long before now.

Though she was regretful about the events of many years ago, Siren understood Lal's actions but wasn't about to surrender her freedom without a fight. Nick assured her the chairman would side with her once he understood the facts. Lal's mate had tried to kill her, after all.

The chairman's lips pursed, his face a road map to frustration. "Sub-Protector," Whizzar spoke slowly and with deliberate intent, choosing his words carefully. "I studied the Alliance Security file concerning the incident twenty-three years ago." He paused and his eyes shifted briefly to Talon, who remained stoically silent, then back to the helmeted alien.

22

"Your mate was a bounty hunter. Bounty hunting is illegal in the Alliance and has been for over a thousand years." He eased back in his chair, burying his hands in his lap, then continued, "Since your wife was committing a crime at the time of her death, and she was attempting to murder an Alliance citizen, I will not grant you extradition of Sirenna Albright."

Without saying a word, Sub-Protector Lal stood and headed for the exit. Nick was so startled he remained seated, but Talon had jumped to his feet and had his blaster out of his holster, ready to repel an attack.

"SIN, lock the doors," instructed Whizzar. No doubt the System Information Network also secured the room so anyone wishing to use a materializer to transport in or out of the office would be blocked from doing so. Lal was trapped.

Lal almost walked into the twin doors that opened onto the corridor beyond, pulling up short when they failed to open. He then turned back to face the chairman, who had stood, his arms hanging loose at his sides. Whizzar glared at the alien.

Suddenly the sub-protector's muscular frame began to shimmer, became transparent, then faded into nothingness. Somehow, against all odds,

Lal had been transported from the room by a materializer.

Impossible, thought Nick. Yet his eyes said otherwise. He swallowed and slowly rose to his feet. *Siren…he's going to kill Siren.*

5

NICK SAT AT his desk in his quarters reading the information on the terminal screen, his frown growing deeper and deeper with each passing second.

The unaligned planet they were headed for was called Brimstone V. Trading ship captains called it by another name, the Planet of Doom. This was because Brimstone V had once been a thriving mining colony extracting iron, gold, copper, and some essential elements for starship construction found on few Alliance worlds until it was devastated by massive earthquakes caused by the mad web of crisscrossing mine shafts bored through the planet's crust. A penetrating sensor scan of the surface would resemble a map of an anthill.

Over the span of several centuries, catacombs, caves, and habitat pockets the miners constructed that ran for thousands of miles had caused the planet's axis to shift, disrupting the planet's magnetic field.

Tectonic plates beneath the surface frequently shifted, sending waves of energy through the planet's crust, eventually making the surface uninhabitable.

A hundred years ago, the mining ended and finally the earthquakes stopped and the last of the volcanoes became dormant as the planet stabilized.

Before the surface became too unstable to support humanoid life, the surviving population retreated underground. Alliance intelligence claimed the inhabitants were now a race of bounty hunters, but this had never been confirmed. Recent events confirmed this was indeed fact. Sub-Protector Lal and his mate were from this remote world. And now Blaster Squad was about to set course for the so-called Planet of Doom.

Lal hadn't killed Siren, he'd kidnapped her and taken her to Brimstone V.

To add to the potential woes, Head of Security Al-Mok Talon told Nick the Brimstone bounty hunters had also acquired a quantity of the energy field they'd been trying to recover. Talon claimed they were planning to deploy the energy as a weapon against the Alliance.

Nick recalled Mili Pumpel's little knowing smile as Talon spoke of Brimstone V.

He wondered if she secretly hoped he wouldn't come back from this mission, at least not alive. *Had our relationship really ended so badly she wishes me dead*?

Deep down he knew it had been a bad breakup. Some people might even describe it as ugly. But he wasn't about to let Mili have the satisfaction by dying.

Nick didn't believe a word Talon said since he had misled them in the past. The man was a wizard with words. But the information Talon provided did give him and the squad an excuse to launch a risky rescue mission to retrieve Siren. He would have gone anyway, but at least this way, the Alliance was footing the fuel bill. Plasma drives are expensive to operate.

He could have asked his mentor Asia Call to help out but she'd already done enough for them and Nick had grown increasingly uncomfortable with her bailing them out of tight spots. He detested owing anyone anything.

Before they left Alliance Station, Nick asked Chairman Whizzar why he didn't send a navy ship to rescue Siren. Whizzar explained the navy had other priorities at the moment. Rescuing one citizen wasn't an urgent enough matter to divert Alliance Navy starships from their current assignments.

However, Nick suspected any delay would result in Siren's execution and he wasn't about to let that happen.

With or without navy support, he had to try. Bones, Gears, and the Kid said they backed Nick's decision.

The door chime sounded, breaking his concentration. "Yes?" he said. Nick had a bottle of water on his desk beside him. He used the interruption to take a sip of the cool liquid.

"It's me, sir," replied the voice of Gears from the comm speaker attached to the wall over his desk. "I need to speak with you."

Nick had appointed Gears his temporary second in command until they recovered Siren. Normally Gears contacted him over the inter-ship comm system, so coming to his quarters in person was highly unusual. "Okay, Gears, come on in."

The door opened, and after Gears entered, he leaned against Nick's bunk and crossed his arms over his narrow chest. The tech genius' demure image belied the fully capable man who could shoot a *Leever* fox's eye out at a thousand meters. These foxes were capable of achieving speeds of 120 kilometers per hour, even over the roughest terrain.

Given the animals home world was dominated by what Earthers would call dinosaurs, the *Leever* fox had evolved great speed to survive becoming the featured item on the reptile's menu.

Though his ocular implants hid his emotions, Gears' face was flushed and his brow was wrinkled. His lips were tensed into a grim line.

"What is it, Gears?"

"This mission stinks of set-up, sir. And we, meaning me, Bones, and the Kid, aren't very happy about it." He shook his head. "You know we'll follow you anywhere, so we weren't about to let Whizzar think we weren't supporting your decision, but we're thinking someone wants us to rescue Siren on Brimstone V."

Nick grunted. "It's a trap."

Gears winced. "Yes, sir, that was our conclusion too."

"Have we been led into traps before?" Nick asked.

Gears nodded.

"And did we survive?"

Gears nodded again.

"Then we'll be ready for this one, just like all the others."

"That's what Bones said…sir."

"How long until we make the FTL jump?"

"Two hours, approximately, Captain."

Nick thought for a second, then said, "Assemble the squad in the FTL hyper-sleep pod bay in one hour. We need to develop a plan before we make the jump." He eyed the tech genius. "Is the stealth shield operational?"

"Yes, sir. Perfectly."

A slow smile formed on Nick's lips. "Good, then I have a few ideas how we might infiltrate the Planet of Doom."

"I *really* don't like that name, sir."

Nick chuckled. "You scared, Gears?"

"A little?" Gears replied tentatively.

"Good. You should be."

6

GSS Hunter
Fifty thousand kilometers from the Brimstone system
4146.12.5 Galactic

Nick scanned the sensor readings on the screen of the Kid's station from where he stood looking over the Kid's seat back. He grunted. "Yeah, I see what you mean, Kid. They have a lot of ships at the border on this heading."

He stood straight and thought for several seconds before speaking. He realized he really should have drunk more water after he exited the hyper-sleep pod, but his guts were twisted by rising tension, so nothing he ate or drank was likely to stay down. A knot of urgency had settled between his shoulder blades, the pain a reminder of how important this was.

"We could set a new heading and make an elliptical approach to intersect with Brimstone Five's orbit," Nick suggested.

"That will add six weeks to the mission," said Gears from the pilot's seat.

"Yeah, right, *Gearhead*, like you got somewhere better to be?" said the Kid sarcastically.

"The name is Gears…not *Gearhead*…. Captain, will you please order this talking muscle to stop—"

"Knock it off, both of you," snapped Nick angrily. "Siren's life is at stake." He turned his attention back to Gears. "Couldn't we engage the stealth shields and take the shortest route to the target?" Nick looked at Gears, whose cheeks had flushed the color of a ripe, red apple. The tech genius nodded.

"But the stealth shields will not have sufficient power to last for the entire mission. At some point we'll become visible to their scans," explained Gears.

"Bones?" said Nick, turning toward the tall, muscular, Martian-born human seated at the weapons station. Bones was doubling as the engineering officer since Siren had been kidnapped and was probably fighting for her life in the tunnels and catacombs of Brimstone V.

The big man shifted in his seat to face Nick. His swarthy features were deadly serious and his scowl made the Kid and Gears shrivel under his gaze. "Siren is my friend," his deep voice filled the flight deck like a weather front rolling in. "We have to go stealth; then, when our power runs low, we'll fight our way out.

32

"Any delay puts my friend at risk and I'm not going to sit here and say I find any delay acceptable. We have no idea how far ahead that bounty hunter is, but when we catch up, I'm gonna kick his butt and send him to hell."

"Okay, big guy," said the Kid. "Take it down a notch."

Bones stood and his hands balled into fists at his sides, his biceps bulged, and his glare seemed to burn a hole in the younger man.

I better break this up before it gets out of control. "We're a team, gentlemen," said Nick, his eyes flitting between the two men. "Fighting between ourselves isn't going to rescue Siren."

"And *you* knock off the sarcasm," he directed at the Kid. "This is tough enough without you stirring the atmosphere."

The Kid looked away, turning to face the screens on his station. His face was flushed and Nick suspected he was angry, but regardless he'd do his job when the time came. Siren's kidnapping had affected them all.

"Kid, have you completed your detailed long-range scans?"

The Kid cleared his throat. "Yes, Captain. There are four patrol vessels within five million kilometers of our current position. They also have a network of surveillance satellites and early warning markers scattered throughout the system. There are eight planets, two of which are or have been habitable. Brimstone V's surface isn't suitable for humanoid life, but as we already know, the underground chambers have a breathable atmosphere and the temperature below ground is within tolerances. Regardless, once below ground I'd recommend environmental suits.

"The other habitable planet is Brimstone Three. According to the readings, the lifeforms there are similar to the cold-blooded animals of Earth's Jurassic period. Brimstone III has two moons, of which we know very little since no Alliance probes have been deployed to study the planet in detail." The Kid paused briefly to take a sip from a glass of fizzy, dark brown liquid on his station—once, when Bones asked him about the drink, the Kid called it soda pop. Nick had no idea what that was but it smelled far too sweet for his tastes. The Kid continued, "The atmosphere is breathable but the temperature even at the poles is hot enough to cook raw meat to well-done after only a few minutes of exposure."

Nick crossed his arms over his chest. "Okay, so we do what Bones suggested."

Gears looked aghast. "You mean we're going to shoot our way out after we rescue Siren?"

Bones grinned and returned to sit at his station. Nick's gaze shifted to the weapons station following his friend's movements. He was taking far too much joy in shooting things and people these days.

It was time to have that talk with Bones he'd been holding off doing.

"Okay, Gears, after engaging the stealth shields, plot the shortest possible route to Brimstone V and get us under way. I'm going to the galley. I need water and a ham and cheese sandwich." He stopped and stared at Bones, who still had his back to him. "Bones, join me, will ya?"

Bones swiveled to face Nick, his eyes saying he would prefer to stay on the flight deck, but his mouth said, "Okay, boss."

They didn't speak again until they were seated across from each other at the galley table. Nick had a glass of water, a coffee with one sugar, and a ham and cheese on rye bread in front of him. Bones chose a toasted onion bagel with butter and a glass of water.

"So, boss, what's goin' on?" Bones said, lifting the glass of water to his lips and taking a sip.

Nick had taken a bite of his sandwich. He chewed and swallowed, washing it down with a sip of the steaming coffee. The cheese, meat, and bread hit the pit of his stomach like a lead weight and though sweetened, the coffee was bitter on his tongue. He pushed the plate with the remaining sandwich away. He was hungry but couldn't eat. His nerves were on edge.

Too much on my mind, he concluded. "Rocky," he said, using Bones' first name, "I wanted to talk to you about your attitude lately."

Bones arched an eyebrow and his gaze shifted to the table. He hadn't touched his bagel. "I knew this was coming," he said, his voice low.

"Bones," Nick shifted to his preferred squad nickname. "You know I count on your skills with weapons and your loyalty."

Bones nodded but continued to avoid eye contact. "Listen, boss, that piece of crap Kid got under my skin. I lost my cool. I'm sorry."

Nick stifled a smile. "You should apologize to him, not me. And honestly, the Kid can be annoying." He shook his head. "I'm talking about your shoot-first-talk-later actions during the last mission."

Bones brought his head up and locked eyes with Nick. His expression reading puzzled.

"Bones, you do know what I'm talking about, right?"

Bones shook his head, his eyes wide.

Nick considered the possibilities. Bones could be pulling Nick's blaster, or he's lying, or he might not remember pulling his weapon to shoot the girl when he first saw her. Or he might have gone mad, but surely there would be signs?

Nick was worried about his friend. Bones had never acted like this before. He enjoyed combat but he had never fired on unarmed soldiers or civilians until recently.

He eyed the big man seated across the table from him. "Bones, do you remember a man called Obri?"

"Uhhh…no. Should I?"

Nick's guts twisted. "What exactly do you remember about our last mission?"

Bones appeared confused and uncertain. His eyes flitted back and forth and beads of perspiration appeared on his forehead.

Nick realized Bones was over-thinking this. "Bones, look at me." Bones locked eyes again with Nick, but Nick could see nothing in the man's eyes or in his expression that said he was lying. "We left Oslun III…then what happened?" Nick said.

Bones' ruddy complexion became twisted with conflicting emotions. "A void. We discovered a void." The words came with effort.

"Okay, good. Then what?"

"We left the void?" he said after another lengthy pause. He appeared hopeful as if Nick was his teacher and he was the student, responding to a question as if he wasn't completely sure of the answer.

Nick smiled and nodded. "Yes. Yes, we did. Okay, let's finish up here and head back to the flight deck." Bones shrugged, then stuffed half the bagel in his mouth and began to chew loudly.

Hoo, boy, there is definitely something wrong with him. Nick decided he'd better ask Gears to do a medical scan of Bones.

I really wish Siren were here.

7

NICK STUDIED THE image of the decimated, so-called Planet of Doom on the center screen of the copilot's station. The rust-red continents, separated by blackened scars that were all that remained of long ago dried-up bodies of water, were visible under enhanced magnification.

According to the Kid's sensor readings, the decimation of the surface was due to centuries of massive earthquakes and enormous volcanoes that erupted, spewing lakes of burning lava, destroying all life that once thrived on the surface of this world. Choking clouds of noxious gasses spewed into the atmosphere and blocked sunlight from the system's G-type star ensuring life wouldn't take hold any time soon, or maybe ever again.

Doesn't look like the garden spot of the galaxy, thought Nick. "Kid, anyone detected us?" asked Nick.

"No, sir," the Kid replied, his voice edged with tension.

I know how he feels, thought Nick. Due to the knot of tension in the pit of his stomach as they passed security drones and markers and patrol ships, some coming within a few kilometers of their position, he hadn't slept or eaten much over the past few days. Gears had tried to get him to eat a cheese sandwich this morning but he daren't take even one bite. He knew he'd vomit if he did. No, he decided, he would wait to eat until after they'd rescued Siren.

"Kid, any ships in orbit?" He glanced over his shoulder at the Kid, whose attention was focused on the screen at his station.

"Yes. Two."

"Class?"

"Warships, by the look of them, much like the one that attacked us in the Earth system," replied the Kid.

"We can take 'em," piped up Bones from the weapons station. "They don't have the firepower to repel our attack."

He was right, of course. "No, Bones, not now. We shoot when we have to, not before," said Nick, shifting in his seat to look at Bones, bent over the tactical screens on the weapons station.

Gears had run a medical scan on Bones and the results were inconclusive. His overall health was very good but the chemicals in his brain seemed out of balance, and the receptors were off somehow, too. Thankfully there was no evidence of the device that had been discovered surgically implanted in the late Obri's frontal lobe. The device interfered with Obri's reason and impulse control. Similar things had been happening to Bones, so Nick really needed Siren to determine the reasons for Bones' actions.

But until Siren was recovered, he'd need Bones' skills on the surface, so Nick would have to take a chance and take Bones with him.

"Any signs of the energy field we're looking for?" Nick asked, referring to the stolen energy field that generated more power than a star. The Alliance had hired Blaster Squad to locate and recover the field before a hostile enemy weaponized it, and that mission remained as yet uncompleted. Every time they'd been close, the field seemed to be just beyond their grasp.

"Traces," said the Kid. "But the readings are inconclusive. I'd say, if it's there, then it's deep underground and surrounded by something capable of blocking sensor scans."

Makes sense, thought Nick.

His secondary mission was to gain access to the energy field and try to recover as much evidence of its whereabouts as possible. The risk would grow the deeper they went into the planet, but risk was a mercenary's business.

"Kid, any life signs?"

"Plenty, sir. Underground, as we expected. None on the surface." He grunted in frustration. "But there is no way to determine which one is Siren. The bounty hunters read as humanoid, very similar to Earthers. The differences are barely measureable. Though the sensors are able to distinguish male from female."

Nick looked thoughtful for several seconds. They could depend on the optical scanners built into their helmets, but he decided to go a different way and use the hand held units. "Program the hand scanners to read their physiology and whether they're male or female. At least we'll have something to work with to find Siren in those tunnels. And make sure you include information about the energy field in case we discover where it might be."

"It's going to be difficult to avoid contact with patrols in there," said the Kid, peering hard at the screen.

Russ Crossley

"I mean, if they have any. They may think they're impenetrable. There is a lot of movement in those tunnels but it might be normal and not armed patrols."

Nick gave the Kid a withering look. Every solider knows there is no such facility that is one hundred percent secure. Never has been, never will be. "Can you generate a map with a search grid?" asked Nick.

The Kid looked at Nick, long strands of black hair falling across his stubble-covered face. He hadn't shaved in a few days. "Yes, sir."

Nick nodded. "Gears, when will we achieve orbit?"

Gears said they should be in orbit within the hour once he'd completed his calculations to avoid the bounty hunters' patrol vessels and satellite detection grid. These aliens were cautious in the extreme, fortifying his belief they'd have patrols in the mining tunnels and catacombs. They'd be ready for a fight, especially since Sub-Protector Lal knew Siren was a high-value asset to Blaster Squad.

After the Kid produced the search grid—and downloaded an e-version into a portable hand scanner—he, Bones, and Nick retreated to his quarters to study the map and determine how they would approach the rescue operation.

Part of the plan was Gears would stay behind to monitor the stealth shields' power levels, and in case the bounty hunters began to suspect they'd been infiltrated. And he would transport them out if the operation went bad. What Nick didn't tell any of his squad: regardless if the operation failed, he'd be staying behind to find Siren. No way was he leaving her in the hands of the kidnappers.

Nick's heart became heavy and his mood darkened the more he studied the intricate tunnels, catacombs, and structures beneath the planet's surface.

Given the level of security, the complexity of the underground tunnels, and the number of armed vessels in the system, it was no wonder the Alliance Navy didn't want to take on these guys. The potential for a major battle with tremendous loss of life on both sides with very little strategic reward seemed incredibly risky.

There was very little chance a straight-on attack would capture or kill every bounty hunter given the web-like structures where they could hide.

The only way, it seemed, to defeat these bounty hunters was for the navy to destroy the planet, killing an entire civilization.

Or send in small teams of mercenaries or Special Forces to conduct surgical strikes against their leadership and critical, high-value targets. But the chance of success was deemed somewhere between very small to no chance at all.

"Just because they live underground doesn't mean they don't have a day and night cycle," offered Bones.

Nick nodded. While he wanted to transport into those tunnels immediately and fight his way to wherever Siren was being held, they needed more information. Bones was right, they had to sleep sometime. However they measured day- versus night-cycle in a society, they might have fewer patrols during the night, though somehow Nick doubted it given the level of security they'd seen so far. *But do I take the chance and wait to see how they deploy resources throughout a full day-cycle?*

"Gears, how long is the planet's rotation?"

"Thirty-two hours," replied the tech genius without hesitation.

Nick considered his options for several seconds, then said, "If we assume they based their day- and night-cycles on the planet's rotation of thirty-two hours when they went underground, then if we orbit for that long, we'll have some idea how they deploy resources—specifically, where and at what time."

He cleared his throat. "I'm proposing we don't wait but take a chance and transport to the tunnels once the Kid determines where there are the lowest number of lifeforms. This will lessen, but not eliminate, the chances of a firefight. Thoughts?"

The Kid grunted. "I will have those coordinates for you in ten minutes."

Well, at least he's in, thought Nick.

"I say let's go," said Bones, his ruddy features a grim mask of determination.

"I'm still staying here, right?" asked Gears, his voice cracking. Nick couldn't help but smile.

"Yes, Gears, we need you here. You'll have to pull our butts out of the fire if things go bad."

Bones and the Kid exchanged a glance and shared a grim chuckle.

"Okay, then we'll reconvene in the materializer room in ten minutes. I want everyone in full battle environmental suits—including you, Gears—fully armed with blaster rifles and pistols. We'll only kill if we have to, but we are either going to rescue our friend Siren or we are going to die knowing we did our best." His three friends nodded, their faces grim masks of determination.

Words for my tombstone, if there's anything of me left to bury, thought Nick.

8

Pathal Continent, Sector 47
Brimstone V
4146.12.21 Galactic

As THE MATERIALIZER beam released him, Nick scanned the area around them, his blaster rifle at the ready. Bones' and the Kid's suit lamps penetrated the dimly lit tunnel, fully illuminating the curvature of the wall to Nick's left. The solid beam of white light from his suit lamp did the same to the wall to his right.

"You read us, Gears?" Nick said softly into the suit comm in his helmet.

They'd donned their armored environmental suits complete with the helmets. The sensor readings showed the atmosphere in the tunnels was breathable for humanoids but Nick wasn't taking any chances. They would need their facilities unimpaired for the duration. The environmental suits were, in his view, a necessary precaution.

"Loud and clear, sir," Gears voice said over the comm.

Nick didn't reply. They'd agreed to have check-in every ten minutes until they were ready to transport back to the *Hunter* or if the situation became untenable.

Of course, Nick hadn't told his team that his definition of untenable was more flexible than theirs.

Reluctantly, Nick had agreed to allow Gears to use the materializer to transport them to new coordinates within the system of tunnels if they became surrounded. Surrounded fit Nick's definition of untenable, provided there was no place to escape to.

"Bones, which way do we go?" Bones had an eidetic memory so he had memorized the grid map the Kid had made of the tunnels. According to the readings, these tunnels were the most sparsely populated. And Gears had worked out a route that would take them into the most populated area, hopefully without being detected. They decided the best chance of locating Siren would be to kidnap someone of importance and use them as leverage to get the location where Siren was being held. Nick hoped they found Sub-Protector Lal, but the odds were slim they'd find him.

"Left," said Bones, before walking away into the dimly lit tunnel.

48

Nick caught the Kid's eye and nodded toward the back of Bones, who had assumed the point position. Since Bones' arms and legs were composed of a steel alloy covered by skin grafts, he was impervious to low-powered blaster fire, thus more likely to survive a full-on blast of superheated energy from a blaster. Consequently Bones often assumed the point position on any mission involving potential blaster fire. And this mission clearly had that potential.

As their boots steps echoed in the tunnel, Nick scanned the tunnel walls. The walls were smooth and didn't require braces. This meant the drill the miners had used generated high levels of heat to carve through the rock, fusing it into its present curved shape. The tunnel floor was flat but the walls were curved up until they met at the top of the curve at least eight feet over their heads.

They had walked a few hundred yards when they came to a chamber as the tunnel widened. Using the beam from his lamp, Nick determined the room was oval shaped, about sixteen feet across at its widest point. Three other tunnels led off in different directions. Thankfully the room was empty of humanoids. There were three barrels, a plain steel desk, and matching chair near the wall to their right.

"You know what this is?" Nick asked Bones.

"Yeah, boss, two of these tunnels lead to dead ends, probably storage, the third leads to a larger room we suspect is a command and control center given the amount of power lines running to and from it."

Nick was impressed. The Kid had really made a very detailed map of these tunnels and rooms. "How many lifeforms in the command and control room?"

Bones held out his portable scanner and squinted at the tiny screen showing the readings. "Five."

Through the faceplate of his helmet, the big man's brow wrinkled. "We've got company coming from the way we came."

"Confirmed," piped up the Kid. The urgency in his voice made Nick uneasy. "Six lifeforms. The readings indicate there are also six fully charged energy weapons."

Nick's guts tightened and his mouth became dry and metallic. "Gears, you following this?"

"Yes, Captain, with great interest."

I bet. "We may become trapped. Be prepared to transport us to another tunnel." He paused and decided to add, "*Only* upon my signal. Understood?"

"Yes, sir," replied Gears, disappointment in his voice.

"Okay, let's move," said Nick. "Double time."

With Bones leading the way, the three squad members began to trot into the tunnel Bones said was the one leading to the command and control center. After a few minutes, they ran out of tunnel when a wall of solid rock blocked the passageway.

"I don't get it," said Bones. "There shouldn't be a wall here."

"The two groups of lifeforms are converging on our position," said the Kid.

Maybe Gears was right after all. "Gears, get us out of here." *I hate being wrong.*

No reply. "Gears?" Still no reply.

"We've lost contact with the *Hunter*," Nick said glumly. "We're going to have to stand and fight."

Nick's heart beat faster as they fanned out to create some distance between them. "Turn off suit lamps," ordered Nick. The tunnel was plunged into darkness as the beams of light went out. Not completely dark since the stone emitted a soft glow, illuminating the darkness but not more than a few meters in any direction. Nick's eyes quickly adjusted to the change in light level.

Nick drew his blaster and checked it. The indicator showed it was, as expected, fully charged.

He hadn't expected it not to be, but in his experience on alien worlds, he had seen the seemingly impossible become very possible. It didn't take much imagination to believe a fully charged blaster could be drained without them knowing. He had heard rumors of this happening from more than one of his fellow mercenaries during his travels throughout the galaxy.

The strap holding his blaster rifle across his back was reassuring, but in the confined space of the tunnel, a rifle would be unwieldy. Somehow Nick suspected whoever was coming had anticipated this.

Nick's heart beat hard in his chest and his grip on the butt of his blaster tightened as the echo of multiple footsteps filled the tunnel. The sounds were coming from the direction they'd just come from.

Abruptly the footsteps ceased. Nick strained to hear any sounds but heard nothing.

"Place your weapons on the ground," said a high-pitched voice that could be female. He never made assumptions based on such limited information, so the speaker could be male for all he knew.

"No. We're here to rescue our friend. Once we see her, we will surrender our weapons," Nick said over the external speaker of his suit.

There was a pause, then he thought he heard a whispered argument.

Finally the voice spoke again. "Is your friend Sirenna Albright?"

Nick froze, sucking in a breath. *What is happening? Does everyone on this planet know Siren?* "Yes. Do you know where she is?"

"If you lower your weapons, we will talk."

Talking was Nick's preferred method of communication. Shooting didn't resolve much of anything and it could make you very dead, very quickly. "Why should we trust you?"

"Because I am her sister, Sonara Albright."

9

Pathal Continent, Sector 48
Brimstone V
4146.12.21 Galactic

NICK, BONES, AND THE KID holstered their blasters
as Sonara Albright, accompanied by ten armed alien
males and females, came into view around the curve
of the tunnel. The Blaster Squad trio had activated
their suit lamps so everyone could see the aliens
had holstered their weapons. There would be no
unnecessary shooting this time. Nick eyed Bones,
who avoided his gaze. *At least there better not be.*

Nick immediately recognized the resemblance
between Siren and the woman before him. Sonara was
tall and slender like her sister, her complexion pasty
and pale, probably due to the time spent underground.
Her hair was inky black and her eyes were cat like,
also like her sister, but they were a deep sky blue,
reminding Nick of a mountain lake where Asia used
to take him fishing in his younger days. Her hair was
pulled back into a ponytail.

She wore a one-piece black jumpsuit with wide gray stripes down the sleeves and down the legs to the middle of her calves. A zipper ran from the top of the neckline to her narrow waist in the middle of her torso between her modest-sized breasts.

She was attractive and looked far too much like Siren. He'd have to watch himself for signs he trusted her too much. He knew Siren well, but he didn't know this woman.

"Captain Justice. It's a pleasure," Sonara said in a husky voice, her lips parted revealing snow-white teeth, the smile traveling to her eyes. There were dark circles under her eyes. Evidently she hadn't been sleeping much.

Nick offered a wry smile and nodded. "The pleasure is all mine. Did Sub-Protector Lal send you to capture us?" He had no time for pleasantries and he wasn't about to let this woman distract him from his mission.

The smile faded from her angular features as Sonara chuckled grimly. "On the contrary. The people here oppose the sub-protector and his bounty hunters. My mission is to rescue Sirenna and capture Lal." Her eyes shifted to her left as a very tall, muscular male stepped from the shadows.

The alien wore black blast armor, and the butt of a large blaster hung from a holster. Nick noted the blaster was on the alien's left side meaning he was left handed. What was really striking was the emerald green eyes set wide apart in the pale gray, fleshy face. His nose was wide and his mouth generous to the point of being out of proportion with the rest of his features. The ears on the hairless scalp were small and set flat against the sides of his head. A patch of chestnut-brown hair decorated his narrow chin.

"This is Leader Poskin," said Sonara, introducing the alien.

"Nice to meet you," said Nick. He glanced at Bones, who had his hand on the butt of his holstered blaster. He caught his friend's eye and shook his head. Bones, with a look of reluctance, dropped his hand away from the pistol to his side.

"What exactly is going on here?" Nick directed his question at Poskin.

The large man's features remained passive while he began to explain in an unexpectedly high-pitched voice.

Leader Poskin and Sub-Protector Lal had once been members of the ruling council that led the government of Brimstone V.

Lal proposed the formation of a bounty hunter league to raise additional funds when the revenues from off-world mining companies began to steadily decrease as valuable minerals became more expensive to extract. Eventually all mining operations ceased and the population began to suffer.

Poskin proposed other, more peaceful, solutions such as opening new trade routes and setting up new immigration agreements with nearby systems. He feared their world would become the target of criminals through the galaxy if they became known as the bounty hunter planet, but Lal secretly went ahead with his plan. Eventually the truth came out, splitting the government into two factions, one of which supported Lal, the other with Poskin. Tensions grew until civil war erupted.

The war began more than thirty-five years ago. Tens of thousands of people had died on both sides across the planet.

"So, if I understand you correctly, you and Lal are enemies." The alien nodded. Nick shifted his gaze until he landed on Sonara. "And I assume Sonara is a freelance *problem solver,* just as we are."

From the corner of one eye, Nick saw Poskin had turned his head toward Sonara.

"I thought you said these beings were enemies?" Poskin asked Sonara.

Sonara's features remained passive, revealing nothing in her eyes or manner that suggested aggression, but her right hand moved slowly to the butt of her blaster. Poskin didn't appear to notice her subtle movement but Nick saw two of Poskin's soldiers standing behind her visibly tense. Things were going to get out of hand quickly if someone didn't do something to prevent a shootout.

"Leader Poskin, I told you they were probably enemies. These people are not bounty hunters, they are mercenaries here to rescue my sister from Lal." Her eyes flitted to lock briefly with Nick's. "They are not in league with Lal and his rebels."

These guys aren't the rebels? thought Nick. *I wonder who the good guys are here, or if there are any good guys.* In his experience, war has few winners and the dividing line between bad and good is usually a fuzzy line at best.

"Sonara," said Nick, addressing Siren's sister, "I gather you're a freelance merc?" She nodded. "How long have you been working for Poskin and his government?"

"Fourteen months," she said glumly.

"And how is the fight against Lal and his rebels going?"

"Not good," she murmured.

There was more Nick wanted to ask Sonara but, for now, what he needed was any Intel Poskin and his people had concerning the whereabouts of Siren. He wasn't about to become embroiled in these people's civil war. Obviously neither side had an advantage over the other. This was a war of attrition and they could end up being among the victims. No, Nick decided, Blaster Squad wouldn't accept any contract for an everyone-loses contest like this one, no matter how much they were willing to pay.

Seeing Sonara's weary features and the dark circles under her eyes, he figured she no doubt regretted accepting the contract. But a deal was a deal in the mercenary world. You were only as good as your last results, and only hired again based on a successful track record.

Poskin nodded to his soldiers and they lowered their weapons, then he said to Nick, "It is a tradition on our planet to welcome visitors with a meal. Will you join us?"

Nick let a wry grin play over his lips. "Yes to the meal, no to the civil war."

The leader grunted. "This one is perceptive."

"Where is Siren being held?" Nick asked.

"I will take you there but we need to make preparations first. Please follow us to our base," said Poskin, his mouth forming a wry grin.

"Let's go with them," Nick told Bones and the Kid.

As they started down the tunnel where the soldiers and Sonara had appeared—Poskin in front with his soldiers flanking him, Sonara behind Blaster Squad—Bones approached Nick. Speaking in hushed tones he said, "Time may be growing short. And we're out of contact with Gears."

Nick nodded. He was well aware of the urgency, but these aliens didn't seem to want to take no for an answer. He was frankly worried how they'd react if he didn't accept their offer.

Like Bones, it bothered him that Gears hadn't used the materializer to transport them back to the *Hunter* per the emergency protocol. There had to be a dampening field blocking both the materializer beam and their comm units.

Since they had no way of calling in the cavalry, they had no choice at the moment but to follow these aliens to their base.

I'm not going to wait very long to continue searching, so this better be fast food and they better have information about Siren's whereabouts or we're outta here.

After walking for an hour, the tunnel began to widen, spreading out until they came to a cluster of buildings. The ceiling rose over their heads until it disappeared into the shadows. The smooth walls glowed and Nick wondered how this was possible. He considered asking Poskin but decided it didn't matter. He wasn't going to be here long enough care.

"Where are we meeting?" Nick asked, scanning the group of three-story buildings closest to where they stood. They were windowless and appeared to be made of the same material as the walls of the tunnels. "Interesting structures."

"Sir, " said the Kid suddenly, his voice excited. "I've reestablished contact with Gears."

Nick walked away from Poskin and Sonara until he was far enough to not be heard. Bones joined him, their backs to their hosts. He activated his comm's private channel speaking rapidly and in a low voice. "Gears. Status."

Gears responded immediately. "Captain. We have big problems. The stealth shields failed ten minutes ago.

A security satellite has started firing at the *Hunter*. So far, the defense shields are holding and will for a while yet. But two patrol ships are on an intercept course. I estimate I have less than thirty minutes before I must break orbit and retreat." Nick knew all too well what would happen if the *Hunter* failed to escape. *We'd be short a ride out of here.* Using the materializer right now probably wasn't the best option. Besides, they were far from completing their rescue mission.

"When will you have the stealth shields operational?"

"If I'm not under attack, I estimate SIN and I will have the repairs completed in one hundred and ten hours."

Nick paused. "Bones, what do you think?"

"Gears should hide out on Brimstone III to complete the repairs. Once the stealth shields are working again, he can come back for us." The big man shrugged. "We should be able to find Siren before then."

Nick gazed into Bones eyes. The rippling biceps, the military buzz cut, the jagged scar running down the left side of his stubble-covered face belied the intelligent man beneath the warrior's exterior.

It was why Nick was willing to cut the large man some slack. All too often, Bones made constructive suggestions such as this one.

"You get that, Gears?" said Nick softly into his helmet comm.

"Yes, sir," Gears said. "I'm on my way. I'll make contact when I return. More bad news though, sir. The star in this system is experiencing considerable solar storm activity. It means while I'm away, I won't be able to contact you."

"Understood. Signing off."

Now all they had to do was survive the next few days in the middle of a civil war, and somehow rescue Siren from one of the opposing sides without annoying the other side.

Well, this ought to be easy to digest as a piece of spicy Klaskin *pie.*

10

Pathal Continent, Sector 49
Government Base
Brimstone V
4146.12.21 Galactic

THE MEAL OF MEAT—Nick would later generously describe it as fried rat—and tubers that tasted like a cross between a potato and a cucumber, with crisp green and red vegetables that tasted like cardboard soaked in seawater, sat in the pit of Nick's stomach transmitting waves of nausea into the back of his throat in the form of sour bile.

Nick, Bones, and the Kid finally removed their helmets after entering one of the government buildings. The inside was divided into offices and a large room that could easily have accommodated a hundred people comfortably. The air inside the building was breathable but was tinged with a slightly metallic scent Nick didn't recognize.

Before they left the main lobby reception area with its armed security contingent, they and their hosts were required to removed their gun belts and unsling their blaster rifles. The weapons were stored in a room by the entrance containing open shelves. The room wasn't locked but two burly armed guards stood, one on either side of the door.

Sonara explained this was a security measure the aliens enforced because a number of infiltrators posing as some of Poskin's soldiers killed a number of government officials before being killed themselves. It seemed suicide was an acceptable tactic on this world.

"Did you enjoy your meal, Captain Justice?" Poskin asked Nick.

"It was fine, thank you," replied Nick. He looked at the Kid, who had been keeping track of the time. The younger man signaled they had one hundred five hours, fifteen minutes until Gears would return for them.

"Now that we've had our welcome meal, Leader Poskin, I would appreciate knowing where my second in command is being held. We will be leaving immediately to rescue her before our ship returns."

Poskin stared at Nick, his features and eyes unreadable.

He remained silent for several moments as if thinking over his response. A knot in his guts gave Nick the sinking feeling whatever the aliens next words were going to be weren't going to be good news. Poskin finally said, "I regret, Captain, this will be impossible."

Beside him, Bones growled and Nick could feel his friend's anger rise along with the tension in his own body. Nick cleared his throat before speaking. "*Why* is it impossible?"

"We have been trying to get to where Siren is being held since Lal captured her. Sonara will explain."

Nick's glare fell on Siren's sister, whose features were flushed with what Nick recognized as a mix of frustration and anger. "Nick, we know where Siren is being held. It's beneath the ancient Milhath Continent on the opposite side of the planet, in a deep mine shaft from the earliest mining operations several millennia ago.

"The mine was abandoned several thousand years ago when a large volcano nearly a hundred miles in circumference formed near the mine entrance and began erupting.

"The massive explosions spewed burning lava flows to bury many of the mine shafts, some reaching several hundred miles below the surface. The mine shaft Siren's being held in survived this period due to its location near the peak of a nearby mountain.

"The volcano has been dormant since those eruptions, but Lal's scientists claim they have a powerful energy field that would bring the volcano back to life and destroy half the planet if we attacked the mine shaft. Patrol ships loyal to Lal captured a pirate vessel just beyond the border of the system and guaranteed the pirates safe passage in return for a portion of the energy field."

Nick eyed Sonara but her features were unreadable. Was she lying? Was this the energy field they were looking for? *Too many questions. Again,* thought Nick glumly. "Does this energy field generate the power equal to a star?" he asked.

Sonara's eyes flared. "Yes," she said slowly. "How did you know?"

Nick ignored her question. "How do we know Lal hasn't killed Siren already?"

Sonara looked away. "We don't know for sure.

"But the last report stated they were awaiting the return of an important elder who was off world negotiating a major bounty-hunting contract before completing Lal's case against Siren. As far as our Intel can gather, the elder has yet to return."

Nick's eyes narrowed and his heart skipped a beat. "You have someone on the inside, don't you?"

"Yes," Sonara said after her eyes flitted briefly to Poskin's, then back to Nick.

Nick let a slow grin flow across his lips. "And it's Siren, isn't it?"

11

Atmospheric Troop Carrier
Brimstone V
4146.12.22 Galactic

THE PASSENGERS WERE thrown side to side against their seat restraints as the sleekly wedge-shaped troop carrier was buffeted in the swirling atmosphere of Brimstone V. The atmosphere was riddled with eddies of swirling, superheated gases, creating violent updrafts and downdrafts making a smooth flight impossible. Fortunately the troop carrier's gravity compensator had been modified to handle traversing this unstable environment.

Nick winced as the craft dipped due to a sudden downdraft, making the small ship drop slightly, then steady as the compensator made the adjustment. The shoulder straps holding him in his seat pressed into his environmental suit. *I wish my stomach had a modified gravity compensator.* He could still taste remnants of the so-called meat they'd been served at the welcoming dinner from the back of his throat.

Blaster Squad #3 Planet of Doom

Blaster Squad had donned their helmets before boarding, this time at Poskin's suggestion. The leader sat next to Sonara, who was piloting the vessel at the front of the ship. The Kid was seated beside him so Nick leaned over to whisper, "What's Gears ETA?"

"Ninety-two hours, ten minutes," said the Kid, his words clipped and sharp. The Kid didn't approve of these aliens coming with them to rescue Siren. But then, neither did Nick.

"How long until we arrive, Sonara?" he said into his suit comm. His suit comm's programming had been adjusted to allow for a channel compatible with Sonara's comm. At Nick's insistence, he included a reserve comm channel for Poskin but only in the event something happened to Sonara. He didn't trust her or Poskin, so he wanted to maintain control over the conversations when he deemed necessary.

Sonara agreed to Nick's conditions on behalf of Leader Poskin, with the exception they could not listen to the alien's communications. Apparently there wasn't a lot of trust on either side, at least not yet.

Nick suspected, if they got into a fight, everyone's true nature would surface. He hoped alliances would form, but he was probably hoping for too much.

The ship dipped to the right, then dropped sharply.

"We're about to land," said Sonara, her voice thick and raspy. Nick assumed she was struggling to control the vessel.

After a few more sharp shakes and a final hard thump, the ship stopped moving. They were on the ground. Nick loosened the shoulder straps, then slipped them off. Bones and the Kid did likewise. Nick stood and stretched his legs and arms. Nothing was broken or strained, which, given the rough flight, surprised him a little.

"Okay, squad, let's gear up and be ready to move out when our host is ready to go," Nick said. Bones had his blaster rifle slung over his back and his blaster pistol in its holster in record time. The Kid was ready as well when Nick had his weapons ready and tested. Everything seemed none the worse for wear.

Sonara, now wearing one of the full-body armored suits the alien soldiers and Poskin also wore, appeared in the crew compartment.

Nick, Bones, and the Kid were seated in the first two rows at the front of the compartment. Behind them were ten tall, heavily muscled, heavily armed soldiers.

Blaster Squad #3 Planet of Doom

Normally Nick preferred to use only squad members for a clandestine mission such as this, but seeing the condition of the soldier's blaster-scarred armor, he suspected these were elite fighters who would be an asset to the operation so he was secretly happy they were coming along.

"You ready?" asked Sonara, directing her question at Nick.

Unlike the squad's armored visors on their helmets, which were transparent with a shading feature in case they encountered overwhelmingly bright lights, her helmet visor was opaque, obscuring her face, which made him vaguely uncomfortable. He really liked to see the eyes of people he worked beside.

Prior to the mission, Sonara explained the visor shields were designed to allow the wearer to see in even the most subdued lighting and had night vision capability and a full tactical display for the wearer. Nick had helmet envy really bad.

"Yeah," he said. "Let's go."

They followed her to the landing bay door at the rear of the crew compartment, past the still seated soldiers. The large hinged door swung slowly open until it stopped with a crunching sound on the black lava, creating a ramp.

Sonara signaled to Nick and his squad to wait and stand aside to let the soldiers exit ahead of them. She then led the way down the ramp, her rifle unslung and gripped in both hands, ready to use if they were met by a hostile force. She signaled for the ten soldiers to deploy five to each side of the ramp, fanned out ready to repel any potential targets.

She then nodded to Nick for his team to follow. Nick hurried down the ramp, his rifle also unslung and at the ready. Bones and the Kid followed, their weapons also held at the ready. Once on the uneven ground, they formed a triangle, their backs to each other.

"Any signs of opposition?" Nick asked Sonara over the comm.

"None," she replied simply.

Using hand signals, she instructed the soldiers to form into two groups, one on either side of Sonara and Blaster Squad, bracketing them with a phalanx of weapons.

Before taking off, Sonara explained Leader Poskin would stay behind on the ship, acting as a communication relay station between the insertion team and their home base.

Once they were underground, direct contact with their base would be impaired without the vessel on the surface acting as a comm patch.

As if choreographed, they quickly moved out as a unit, the soldiers trotting at a steady pace across the tortured dark landscape. It was night, but two moons in the sky, one smaller than the other, cast a soft white glow across the barren, obsidian landscape. In the distance Nick could see the shattered shell of the volcano rising from the surface, kilometers into the star strewn sky.

Twisted pillars of jagged lava dotted the rocky plain around them, littered with shattered pieces of lava, no doubt evidence of the centuries of earthquakes that tore through the planet during its long period of upheaval. Nick was amazed any humanoid life survived this scene of extreme devastation.

According to his suit's readings, the surface temperature was minus ten degrees Celsius. The poisonous, acidic atmosphere would melt their lungs within minutes of exposure. Nick was glad Leader Poskin required they wear their environmental suits.

After fifteen minutes of quick time marching, they came to what appeared to be a fifteen-meter-high, large steel blast door.

There was no evidence of hinges or latches on the smooth, burnished surface; however, there were jagged score marks across the metal surface evidence of sustained blaster fire. These people had been at war for a long time so it wasn't surprising to see every object they encountered bore the residue of battle.

"Our scans indicate thus far we have not been detected," explained Sonara. "We enter through this door."

"But how?" asked Bones. "There isn't a latch."

Sonara held up a device she'd had attached to a belt around her waist. It reminded Nick of a handheld comm device. She aimed the device at the door and it slide along a track to the left until it disappeared into a slot in the rock. There was no sound.

Nick peered into the blackness beyond the entrance, his heart beating faster and a rush of adrenaline coursing through his system. It was very likely they were about to face a firefight before this was over and some of them would not be returning.

His eyes darted between Bones and the Kid and his grip tightened on the stock of his blaster rifle. Nick had a sinking feeling he might not be coming back from this one.

He hoped whoever made it out brought Siren with them. She was all he cared about right now.

12

Milhath Continent, Sector 79, Mine shaft 47776
Brimstone V
4146.12.22 Galactic

THE ELEVATOR CARRYING the soldiers and Blaster
Squad stopped at the five-kilometer depth with
a slight lurch. Nick was glad he wasn't prone to
claustrophobia given the cramped elevator and the
warm bodies packed too tightly as far as he was
concerned. If they were greeted by weapons fire
when the elevator doors opened, they would all die.
Sonara assured him they would be undetected until
they reached the network of tunnels, but he remained
uncomfortable.

"You can remove your helmets," Sonara said as
the door slid aside, revealing a dimly lit, gradually
widening tunnel leading away from the elevator into
the distance where it disappeared in the shadows.
Like the walls in the tunnels they'd encountered
before, the walls were smooth and glowed softly,
casting an eerie light over the floor and walls.

Nick felt the tension between his shoulders ease when he what he could see of the tunnel was empty. Lal hadn't sent a reception committee.

One of the soldiers to Nick's left stepped from the elevator into the tunnel, a portable scanner in his left hand. He had removed his helmet revealing his brilliant, emerald-green eyes and pale, hairless features. His eyes flitted over the scanner readings as his brow grew more furrowed with each passing second. With his eyes still fixed on the screen, he waved for the others to join him.

The remaining soldiers exited first, fanning out to form a perimeter. They had their rifles at the ready. Sonara had also removed her helmet and she smiled at Nick.

"Well, let's go," she said in a singsong voice.

What's made her so happy? Nick wondered.

Nick, followed by Bones and the Kid, stepped into the tunnel. Disregarding Sonara's assurances, they had not removed their helmets. Bones had his rifle still slung over his back while the Kid held his casually with the barrel pointed at the floor. Nick hadn't bothered to unsling his, either. If there was an ambush, he was sure the soldiers could handle the initial barrage until they could deploy their own weapons to back them up.

Nick was sure Sonara had been briefed about Blaster Squad's capabilities. It wasn't exactly a secret, nor, truth be told, did he want it to be.

He eyed Sonara's lovely features. In contrast to these aliens, she probably knew more about them than all the residents of Brimstone V combined. And it worried him.

"Where to next?" he asked Sonara.

Her smile faded and her eyes narrowed. "Siren is being held in another tunnel five kilometers from here. We will move to the junction between the tunnels, then split into two groups. We may encounter security patrols along the way, but they won't pose much of a threat."

Nick's eyes narrowed and he exchanged looks of uncertainty with Bones and the Kid. "I thought you said they would be able to monitor us after we arrived in the tunnel."

She nodded, her mouth now a grim line of determination. "Of course, but given the size of our force, they will think we're a recon mission, not a rescue mission. Poskin's forces usually attack in greater numbers so they will be unwilling to deploy a large force to engage us until they realize our objective."

"Sir," it was the Kid on Nick's comm. "The energy field is here. The readings are off the scale." Nick acknowledged this new information with a look of understanding at the Kid. The stakes had just gone up. They had a shot at recovering Siren and the energy field in one fell swoop. That was, of course, if everything went as planned.

"Okay, then lead on, Macduff," said Nick. Sonara gazed at him quizzically. Nick chuckled. "It's an old Earth expression meaning…" Actually he had no idea what it meant. It was something Asia said and it seemed appropriate to the current situation.

"Never mind. Sorry." *I really gotta watch using Earth idioms around aliens, especially ones I don't understand myself.*

Sonara grunted and shook her head. She said something into her comm that he couldn't hear on his comm. The soldiers around them looked at each other and shrugged, then went back to scanning the tunnel for potential threats.

Sonara signaled to the soldiers to move in two groups, one on each side of the tunnel, staggered so they could provide covering fire without shooting each other.

Following behind the soldiers, Sonara and the Blaster Squad members would be in the middle of the tunnel, a few paces between them with their weapons ready.

After an hour march, they came to a T-junction. Thankfully they hadn't encountered any of Lal's troops along the way. "Left or right?' asked Bones.

Sonara looked at the solider ahead of them in the tunnel who still held the handheld portable scanner. "Right," the man said without hesitation.

"He's wrong, sir," said the Kid in Nick's comm.

"Hold on, Sonara. We should go left," Nick said.

Sonara turned to face him, her eyes quizzical. "Why would you say that? My man says we should go right."

Nick noted she was on their private channel. She wasn't letting her soldiers in on this conversation. *Maybe I've misjudged her*, he thought. "Your man may be lying. I don't know why, but it's important to check it out." He looked into her eyes. "You said yourself, Lal's people have infiltrated Poskin's before."

"Why does your man think we should go left?" Her eyes flitted briefly to the Kid.

She can hear our communications and yet she said nothing, until now.

"You heard?" he said. She nodded. Nick lips formed a wry smile. "Kid, tell her why we should go left."

"Two kilometers from the junction down the tunnel leading to the left is a concentration of some three hundred humanoids and a strong concentration of the energy field. To the right I detect a hundred humanoids and a concentration of energy signatures emitted by blaster charge packs and other energy weapons of a type I can only guess at. If I were a betting man, I'd say we'd be walking into an ambush if we went to the right."

Sonara pulled her blaster pistol from the holster on her hip and strode to confront the solider holding the hand scanner.

The soldier's eyes widened as he realized she was raising her weapon, intending to fire on him. He dropped the scanner and it shattered on the tunnel floor as he reached for the blaster in his holster. The other soldiers raised their rifles and one of them fired the brilliant beam of energy, striking the traitorous solider in the center of his chest.

Fired from such close range, the beam of high intensity energy caused his chest plate to be compromised and a blackened hole to appear in the center of his chest.

His gloved fingers lost their grip on his partially drawn pistol until he dropped his weapon. It skittered across the tunnel floor until it stopped against the upward curve of the wall. The man then sank to his knees, his mouth open in a silent scream, rust-brown blood trickled from the left side of his mouth. His eyes were a wild fusion of shock and pain.

Finally, as the beam released him, the now dead man fell forward to land facedown, unmoving, a cloud of blue smoke wafting over his corpse. The sickening odor of burned flesh filled the tunnel.

Nick stood frozen, unable to speak, gaping at the scene of sudden violence and death exacted so swiftly. No trial. No determination of guilt or innocence. No jury of your peers. Just an automatic death sentence carried out efficiently and with finality. It was primal justice. And Nick didn't like it.

"What the hell was that all about?" Nick spat his words, not bothering to disguise or suppress the anger burning in his gut.

Sonara didn't reply to Nick's question; instead, she approached the dead soldier and used her right foot to roll him onto his back. The dead man's eyes and mouth were open and his features were blanched and ashen. The blood on the left side of his mouth had stopped running.

"He was a traitor. His name was Taxon. I expect he was a spy working for Lal."

Nick's heart froze. "You knew this?" She nodded, her eyes fixed on the dead man. Watching her Nick realized this man had meant something to her. The tension in his body receded. "Was he a friend?" he said his voice gentle.

A brief smile passed over her eyes and lips. "Yes, he was my lover. We were as the peel of an apple, very close." Her last words were whimsical and surprisingly playful. She was revealing a different side of her nature in this most vulnerable of moments.

He saw a flash of remorse cross her eyes. "I have to ask. I'm sorry, but why kill him now?"

Sonara sighed and turned away from her dead lover to face Nick. "I'd been using him to funnel disinformation to Lal. Poskin asked me to help feed false intelligence to their enemy. I did…" Her next words caught. She cleared her throat. "Unfortunately, I fell in love, too often the consequence of such a scheme." Her eyes drooped at the corners.

"He was leading us into a trap designed to kill us all." She paused and her brow wrinkled as her cat-like eyes became hard points. "Including me," she finished.

"Yes, but why now?"

Her eyes became quizzical. "What do you mean? I thought it obvious. To save us, of course."

Nick drew his pistol and pointed it at the center of Sonara's chest. His eyes flitted to where Bones and the Kid stood nearby. They had withdrawn their weapons as well and had them pointed at the nine remaining soldiers. "I'm having trouble with the convenience of all this," said Nick, "I think there is far more to your story. Something you're concealing from us." He nodded toward her gun belt around her waist. "Take off your gun belt and lay it on the floor. And order the soldiers to lay down their weapons."

From the corner of his left eye, Nick detected movement. Bones fired his blaster, the whine filling the cavernous space, and two soldiers crumpled to the ground. Glancing at the incapacitated soldiers, Nick saw they were breathing. Bones had set his blaster on its non-lethal setting. *Well, how about that, a Gegsit cat really can change it spots.*

The remaining soldiers lay their rifles and pistols on the tunnel floor. "Step away," ordered Bones in a his deep voice, motioning with his blaster.

They complied but their eyes burned with rage. Nick knew, if they managed to recover their guns, Bones and probably him and the Kid would be ash in seconds.

Sonara gazed at him with placid eyes. "You going to shoot me, too?" she asked. "I could use the rest," she said mockingly.

Nick's eyes narrowed. Using his thumb, he moved the slider on the butt of his blaster to the lowest setting. "No, I'm reserving disintegration for you. Unless…" He let his words peter out as he raised the pistol to take aim at her head.

Her eyes flared and she swallowed hard. "You seem to think I know something…important."

"Oh, you do, Sonara, you do. And you're going to tell me what I want to know."

Sonara's shoulders eased and she crossed her arms. She obviously didn't think he'd fire. *And she'd be right*, he thought. *But only for so long*. "What do you want to know?" she asked a sardonic grin on her lips.

"Your sister is working with Sub-Protector Lal." She nodded. "And Lal's is the legitimate government." The grin faded but she nodded again, though this time with hesitation. "Which means you work for the rebels, not the government. Poskin and his rebels intend to overthrow the government. He is the leader of the bounty hunter league, not Lal.

Disguised as a bounty hunter, Lal kidnapped Siren to draw us here, hoping you would help them defeat the league and capture Poskin."

"Yes," she said between gritted teeth after a short pause, her eyes searching his. "How did you know?"

"I didn't until just now," said Nick with a grim smile.

This is gonna get really interesting.

13

NICK DEPRESSED THE firing stud on his blaster, careful to direct the beam into the center of Sonara's chest. Her eyes widened briefly in surprise, then like overly whipped mashed potato, she sank to the tunnel floor unconscious. She was breathing, so Nick knew she was alive. Even set on the stun setting, the blaster still delivered considerable force. He was relieved she was alive. He didn't need the blood of Siren's sister on his hands.

"How long will they be out?" Nick asked the Kid.

"I'd estimate six hours, maybe slightly more, boss."

Nick gazed at Bones, who appeared irritated, his brow wrinkled and his lips pursed. "What's wrong, Bones?"

The big man shook his head. "This was too easy. Almost like they wanted us to stun them."

Nick nodded. "Exactly my thoughts as well, big guy." He turned to face the Kid. "Will our suit comms reach other comms set to receive the Blaster Squad-only frequency?"

The Kid's brow furrowed. "Yeah, I suppose so, but they'd have to be in range. We're too deep below ground if you're thinking we'd be able to reach Gears. Even from the planet's surface, the signal wouldn't get through."

Nick let a small smile flow over his lips. "Justice to Siren, come in."

Nothing. He wondered if he'd made a mistake. *Maybe I was wrong about Sonara and Poskin.* Maybe the rebels were holding Siren captive after all.

"Nick? Is that you?" It was Siren, her tone one of excitement.

"Yes, Siren. I'm here with Bones and the Kid. Are you okay?"

"Yes, I'm fine. How far away are you?"

Nick looked at the Kid. "Hi, Siren, it's the Kid. We can be at your coordinates in an hour, maybe less." He gazed at Nick and tapped the side of his helmet to indicate he was switching to a private frequency. "Sir, we don't know if she's being coerced. I'd recommend taking the precaution of not telling her our exact position, at least for now."

Nick nodded, then switched his comm back to the Blaster Squad frequency. He agreed they needed to be cautious. Siren could have been compromised. How had she known to monitor the Blaster Squad-only frequency? It was as if she'd been waiting for his signal.

Nick looked at the Kid as he spoke. "We have your position. It won't be long. We'll have you back home soon. Justice out." He switched the comm back to the private frequency Gears had set up between Bones, the Kid, and himself. They would also be able to contact Gears without anyone monitoring their conversation.

"We don't have her position exactly," said the Kid, who exchanged a worried glance with Bones.

Nick nodded. "I know that but she doesn't. If she's being coerced, whoever is holding her won't either." He turned to face the tunnel to their right. With his right hand, he indicated the dimly lit tunnel. "We're going in there to find Siren and rescue her, just as we intended from the beginning."

"But, boss, I thought we established that way was the wrong choice. We'd be walking into an ambush," said Bones.

Nick arched an eyebrow at Bones. "And how does an ambush work?"

The Kid grunted and Nick looked at him. "Go ahead, Kid."

A wry grin played across the Kid's nut-brown Mediterranean features. "An ambush only works if those being ambushed are unaware they are walking into one."

Nick chuckled. "Exactly. In this case, we know there will be an ambush if we enter the right tunnel. So, we go in prepared for an attack and disrupt the rebels attack before they attack us."

"Yeah, right," snorted Bones derisively. "Sounds simple when you put it that way, boss, except there are three of us and a hundred of them. I'd say no matter how you slice the *Mokitry* pie, we're not going to win in a straight-up fight against a hundred heavily armed rebel soldiers."

Nick eyed the thickly muscled man he trusted with his life. His eyes narrowed to fine slits and his gripped tightened on the butt of his blaster he had holstered after shooting Sonara. "I know I'm asking a lot, but I need you guys to trust me. I think we will overcome the rebels before they kill us." He paused, his eyes darting between the two men. This mess was getting really confusing. Who were enemies and who were allies seemed to be shifting under them like sand in a windstorm.

He hoped his friends would go along for the ride. "Are you with me?"

"You bet we are, sir," replied Bones, a wide grin splitting his unshaven features.

After half an hour moving swiftly down the tunnel, they came to a stop when the Kid's handheld scanner detected a force of twenty-two lifeforms gathered in the tunnel near section 81. The readings indicated the lifeforms were armed with energy weapons.

Nick dropped to his haunches as soon as they heard the echo of mumbled voices ahead in the tunnel. Bones and the Kid were crouched low, their blaster rifles in their hands, their bodies pressed against the tunnel wall one on either side ahead of Nick in the tunnel. "Do you wish me to go ahead, sir?" whispered the Kid.

"Yes, but be careful not to be seen."

Gears had provided special shielding built into their suits to prevent sensor scans from detecting them. The shields dispersed the scanners' signal, making it seem as if there was nothing there to detect. It wasn't stealth technology as they'd seen installed in spacecraft, they were still visible, but the shielding did provide an element of surprise.

Nick hoped no one else had developed such technology, or the days of the sneak attack were going to be tossed into the trash recycler along with the chemical rocket.

"Acknowledged," replied the Kid.

Nick watched the younger man until he disappeared into the gloom farther down the tunnel. The Kid would eventually sling his rifle across his back again and drop to his stomach. He'd then crawl across the tunnel floor, trying to stay out of the soft glow of the walls, trying to stay in the shadows until he could see what was ahead.

Nick's heart rate increased with each passing second they were out of contact with the Kid. A trickle of perspiration ran down his spine. The air inside his environmental suit was becoming rank with his stale sweat.

Bones glanced back at him and nodded his head toward the tunnel. *He wants to go in with guns blazing.* He shook his head and turned his attention back to the empty tunnel. He thought he heard a brief hum of blaster fire, then silence again. *I must be imagining it.*

After what seemed like an eternity, but according to his chronometer was no more than fifteen minutes, there was a brief flash of movement that made his heart skip a beat. He hefted his rifle and aimed into the darkness. "Sir. It's me," said the Kid, his voice sounding strained as if he were gasping for air.

The Kid appeared from the gloom, stumbling close to the wall. His blaster rifle was gone and a bloody gloved hand was pressed against his right torso. Through his suit visor, Nick could see the young man's ashen complexion and the pain in his eyes.

14

Milhath Continent, Sector 81, Mine shaft 47776
Brimstone V
4146.12.22 Galactic

BONES RELEASED HIS rifle, and since it was tethered
to his environmental suit, it swung to his side as he
rushed to grab the Kid before he fell. Bones wrapped
an arm around the Kid's waist and threw the Kid's
arm over his shoulder. He then helped him to a spot
near the wall. Nick eased the wounded man to the
tunnel floor. The Kid winced as he settled on the floor.

Bones shifted his gaze to Nick. His eyes contained
raw fear, something Nick had never seen in the big
man. "It's gonna be okay, Bones," Nick whispered.

"Are you sure?" said a familiar voice.

Nick's heart skipped a beat and he froze, with his
hand moving instinctively to the blaster pistol on his
hip. *Siren.*

"Place your weapons on the ground," said a deep
male voice Nick also recognized.

Lal. Nick imagined a firefight would be nasty and
bloody, but mostly their blood.

Surely Siren wouldn't attack us? "What if we refuse?" Nick asked, his eyes darting to Bones, who stood with his legs apart, his hand resting on his blaster. He looked down at his rifle, then to Nick. They were on the same wavelength. He shook his head slightly to indicate Bones shouldn't take any action until Nick said so.

Nick dropped to gaze at the Kid, who had passed out. Blood seeped from the wound in his side and his head had dropped to his chest. He was still breathing but he wouldn't be for much longer if he didn't get medical attention soon. And Siren, with her medical training, was just beyond those shadows.

"Then you will be captured using as much force as is required," said Lal.

Nick considered the sub-protector's words carefully. *Translation: they don't want to kill us, but they will if they have to.*

Nick dropped to his haunches next to the Kid. He shook the younger man awake. The Kid looked at Nick, his eyes hurting and his breathing coming in gasps. "Kid, what happened?"

"I heard a noise…close…too close…I fired…shot me…" His eyes rolled up and he passed out again. Nick was certain the younger man's life expectancy could be measured in minutes.

He had to do something to end this stalemate.

Nick rose to his feet. He pulled his blaster from the holster and let it fall to the floor. He then unslung his rifle and dropped it as well. He looked at Bones and indicated he should do the same. Bones gave him a pained expression but he did as instructed.

"Okay, Lal, we surrender." He could have demanded they treat the Kid's injuries or they wouldn't comply, but then they'd be dead and the Kid with them. This way there was a chance, and besides, being dead was no way to make a point.

A group of armed soldiers appeared from the shadows. They were dressed in the same purple body armor Lal wore when Nick first encountered him back at the Alliance Station. They moved quickly to gather up their weapons, including the ones next to the unconscious Kid. Nick noticed how pasty the Kid's features looked.

Siren appeared from behind the soldiers. But where was Lal? He seemed fearless when Nick met him, not one to avoid confrontation and send others to do his work. He wondered if he'd misjudged the alien leader.

Nick's eyes narrowed as he saw Siren staring at him. She appeared unharmed. She walked toward him, her blaster holstered and no signs of a rifle.

She wore her favored outfit of a one-piece faux leather suit that was far more flexible than it appeared since she was a martial arts expert. She wore no blast armor. Her long, coal-black hair was pulled into a tight ponytail that swung as she walked.

"Hello, Siren," said Nick as she stopped before him, gazing unblinking at him.

She didn't say a word as she withdrew the blaster, and before he could react, she fired. The last thing he heard before the darkness engulfed him was the whine of the blaster energy beam.

15

Location unknown
Date unknown

NICK GROANED AS he opened one eye. The room around him began to spin and his stomach twisted as if it were in a vice. Squeezing his eyes closed, he clutched his stomach and tasted sour bile at the back of his throat. *Damn, I feel like crap.* His helmet had been removed.

"I'm really sorry, Nick."

"Siren?" His voice was cracked and dry as a desert in his own ears.

"Yes." A hand pressed on his right shoulder. "Calm down and take deep breaths in through your nose, then out your mouth. Slowly at first. Hold for second or two, then release and repeat. Your heart rate will slow and the nausea will gradually subside." He did as she instructed and immediately began to feel better. "Good," she said soothingly.

Nick managed to rise from his side, where he'd been lying on something soft, to a sitting position.

"Draw your legs up, then place your head between knees and continue with the steady breathing. The dizziness will disappear soon."

After several minutes, Nick finally managed to open his eyes. Pain shot across his forehead; the overhead lights were bright. He blinked repeatedly until his vision began to clear and the pain eased. He scanned his surroundings.

He sat on a bed, a cot really, with a navy-blue blanket and a pillow. The room appeared to be about six meters by six meters in size, with forest-green unadorned walls and no windows. Across the six-meter-square room, set against one wall was a burnished steel table and a single, matching armless chair. There was a steel door with no handle recessed into a metal doorframe that Nick assumed was locked from the outside. This was a prison.

"Bread and water for dinner?" he asked Siren, who gazed at him with warm, sensitive eyes.

The compassion faded from her gaze as a frown darkened her features and her eyes narrowed. "How can you joke at a time like this?"

"At a time like *what*?" he said angrily.

"You know perfectly well," she said, surprise evident in her tone.

Nick chuckled grimly. "All I know for sure is Bones, the Kid, and I came here to rescue you from Lal, and for some reason I've yet to understand, you shot me."

Her face contorted in confusion. "I did not. I've been locked in this room since Lal kidnapped me and brought me here. I don't even know where here is." She sighed and shifted her bottom on the bed to allow him extra room. "I was referring to the execution."

"Execution?" Now it was his turn to be confused. "Siren, tell me what the hell is going on."

Siren dropped her eyes to the blanket. "You and the others have been convicted of treason. You're due to be executed in a few hours. And I didn't shoot you," she protested.

"Treason?" Nick moved off the bed, standing on shaky legs, pressing one hand against the wall beside the bed to steady himself. "How can I be convicted of treason if there wasn't a trial? A treason against who? Lal?"

Siren shook her head as she too stood and crossed her arms over her chest. "No, of course not. Sub-Protector Lal represents the rebels fighting for freedom from the tyrant Poskin and his oppressive government.

Poskin and his allies are responsible for the League of Bounty Hunters, secretly funding their training and equipment in return for fifty percent of the proceeds. They aren't just bounty hunters, however. They are also assassins who have murdered a number of prominent corporate executives throughout the Alliance. And they tried to kill me over twenty years ago."

Nick considered her words for several moments. "The person who attacked me wasn't you," he said at last.

She looked at him quizzically. "What do you mean?"

"I think it was a duplicate of you. A doppelganger." He shook his head. "I don't know how and why, but someone is able to make exact duplicates of living beings."

Her eyes went wide, registering her surprise. "Robots? Androids?"

"No, I don't think so. I think something far more insidious. A shapeshifter of some kind maybe, or more likely an organic clone, artificially created in a laboratory using our own DNA. Something we have never seen before."

"So any one of us could be duplicated… impersonated by these *things*?" Siren said, the surprise evident in her voice.

He nodded. "You, me, Bones, the Kid—any of us could be an imposter. How long this has been going on is unknown. Anyone in the Alliance could be a doppelganger, from the most powerful to the poorest worker on the most backwater planet in the galaxy."

Siren grunted and he knew immediately she wasn't a duplicate. Her inner resolve that made her such a formidable second in command had once again surfaced. "Of course, but if you want to conquer someone, you don't use beings on backwater planets."

Nick offered her a grim smile as he stepped away from the wall, his strength improving with each passing second. "No, you're right, of course. Whizzar could be a duplicate and could have been one when he engaged us to recover the energy field. These doppelgangers may have plans for that energy field. Dangerous plans."

The steel door swung open, the hinges creaking loudly. Lal, accompanied by two soldiers armed with blaster rifles, stepped into the room. His cold gaze scanned them and the room.

"Are you ready?" he said, directing his words at Siren. She nodded.

This is getting so confusing, thought Nick. *I have no idea what side is what. But at least they both have the same story.*

"Where we goin'?" asked Nick.

Lal arched an eyebrow at Nick. "Well, Captain Justice, *we* are going to war with Leader Poskin and his corrupt government. And you and your Blaster Squad mercenaries are joining our side."

"What about the executions?"

Lal shifted his gaze to Siren and a grim smile played across his lips. "What have you been telling him?"

Siren shrugged. "Well, it's true. Sort of."

Nick's eyes narrowed and he cursed under his breath. "What is she talking about, Lal?"

"Leader Poskin has announced a bounty on you and your squad. Dead or alive, I might add." He shrugged. "I'm certain he would prefer the latter."

16

Milhath Continent, Sector 77, Mine shaft 47776
Brimstone V
4146.12.23 Galactic

NICK HAD DONNED his armored environmental suit but left off his helmet. His weakness from the aftereffects of being stunned had finally dissipated. He once again felt strong and his confidence had returned. However, he remained uncertain about this operation to stop Poskin, who may or may not be a corrupt leader. He still wasn't a hundred percent certain who was telling the truth, or even if they knew the truth themselves. With doppelgangers running around, this planet's civil war had become a seriously disjointed mess.

Nick crouched low with Siren beside him, her breathing shallow. He wasn't convinced this was the real Siren, but for now he would operate under the assumption she was his second in command.

Bones was to his left, also without his helmet.

They were in a newly dug tunnel, one of twenty surrounding the three hundred humanoids registering on the Kid's hand scanner that Nick now held, and of course the energy field that generated a more powerful signal than ever. In fact, the energy signature of the field seemed far too high for humanoid life to survive being near for long. Siren assured him it was safe. It felt like the old days. *Good times*.

They were awaiting a signal from Lal to burst through the remaining rock separating them from the complex beyond. He used his suit lamps, as did Bones, to illuminate the tunnel since the glowing rock did not seem to be present in these strata. The newly formed tunnel smelled of ozone, a remnant of the device used to create it. The digging device was no bigger than a baseball bat, making it portable. It generated a wide beam of concentrated energy that dissolved rock into a sugar-like consistency. It would certainly cut through flesh as if it were a wet sponge if used as a weapon. Each team had one of the devices and an accompanying technician who knew how to use it.

The Kid remained behind at the rebel base with Lal's team of emergency medical techs, who administered to his wounds.

They said he would live, though, due to the extreme loss of blood, he was too weak to accompany them.

Nick agreed to help Lal after Siren explained she and her sister had indeed been in constant contact. Together they planned to stop Poskin, and though it went against his base instincts, he decided to support Siren's decision to help her sister in her mission. It might provide them an opportunity to capture the energy field, thereby completing at least part of their mission of Chairman Whizzar. Bones said he'd support whatever Nick decided was best.

"There's the signal," Siren whispered words came through the comm.

Nick gripped the holds on the blaster rifle tighter and his heart began to beat faster. Even after years as a mercenary, a potential firefight still gave him a rush of adrenaline. At times like this, he was like a five-year-old who drank too much sugary soda.

The tech with the hand drill stepped up and aimed the business end of the conical-shaped device at the wall of rock in front of them and paused. He then glanced at Siren, who nodded. Nick shielded his eyes with one hand just in time before the tech dropped his eye shield, adjusted his aim slightly, then fired.

Russ Crossley

Nick could smell the increased ozone and feel the heat of the cutting beam as it enveloped the rock, dissolving it as he watched. It fell into dust at their feet and the lit cavern beyond appeared. A band of four unarmed aliens gaped at them as they rushed through the newly created doorway.

Five other openings appeared around the cavern and soldiers poured through, joining them. The four aliens gapped at the collected soldiers their expressions fearful and their eyes wide as saucers of sour Mok juice.

"Don't move," ordered Siren, approaching the nearest alien woman, a slender female wearing a loose-fitting gray shirt and gray pants. Open leather sandals adorned her narrow feet.

The alien's ruby-red hair flowed across her narrow shoulders and her emerald-green eyes set wide apart in the pale gray fleshy face flitted between Siren and Nick. Her nose was hooked and her mouth generous. "What is going on?" she said in perfect Galactic English. Her breath smelled strongly of something reminiscent of garlic.

Nick looked into the woman's eyes and realized she really hadn't expected to be confronted by a band of rebel soldiers. Her surprise was no deception. "Where are the guards?" he asked.

"Guards?" she said in a dismissive tone. "There are no guards here. We are a community of intellectuals and scientists. We have nothing of value to guard."

Nick lowered his rifle and turned to face Siren. "What the hell is going on?" He let his frustration seep into his voice.

Siren appeared as confused as he felt. "Nick, I'm sorry, I don't understand. Our intelligence reported this was a military base…" She hesitated and raised her portable scanner. Her almond-shaped yellow eyes flitted across the readout. "The energy field readings have flat-lined."

Nick looked over his shoulder when the alien woman snorted derisively. "Of course your readings have flat-lined. The field was moved to a secret laboratory for further testing," she said dryly as if they were too stupid to understand. "And before you ask, we have no idea where the secret laboratory is located. We are scientists, not secret agents."

Nick smiled to himself. He turned back to face her. "What is your name?" he asked.

"Dr. Oilil," she replied arching one thin eyebrow.

Nick offered her a tight, mirthless smile. "Well, doctor, I may not believe you about the location of the energy field, but it isn't important at the moment.

I want to know where Leader Poskin is…and don't try to tell me you don't know where he is. I know you do."

The arrogant expression on the alien woman's face disappeared and her brow wrinkled as her eyes the color of lemons narrowed. "I will not tell you *anything* about Leader Poskin," she said, determination and defiance in her voice.

Nick slung his rifle over his back and drew his blaster pistol. The woman visibly stiffened but Nick, instead of aiming the gun at her, focused on one of her two companions—a shorter alien female with narrow, beady eyes. Though he didn't know anything about this race's physiology, she appeared to be younger than Dr. Oilil. A daughter or a niece, perhaps?

The younger woman's pleading, fearful eyes shifted between Dr. Oilil and the gun. Beads of perspiration appeared on her forehead and she began to tremble.

"Wait," said Oilil, "please," she added, pleading with him.

Nick holstered his weapon. "So where is Poskin?" He gazed steadily into her eyes. "I'm not going to ask again."

"He's at the commerce building," she said softly. Her eyes welled with tears.

Nick looked at Siren. "Where?"

She nodded toward a tunnel left of their position.

Nick withdrew his blaster again and pointed it at Dr. Oilil, who sucked in a breath, her eyes registering her surprise. Nick depressed the firing stud and a beam of energy engulfed the woman. She stiffened, then dropped to the ground as the beam released her. Bones quickly did the same to each of Oilil's companions. All three aliens lay at their feet. Their chests were rising and falling, meaning they were still breathing. It was as if they were asleep, but he knew from personal experience the dreamless sleep after being stunned. When you awoke, the sense of lost time was discomforting.

They'd wake up in a few hours with a bad headache but hopefully suffer no lasting effects. Regardless, Nick didn't want the killing of unarmed civilians on his conscience if it could be avoided.

"Let's go," he said, moving toward the tunnel.

"You know, Nick, you really know how to play your cards," said Siren as she hurried after him. Bones and the troop of rebels followed after them.

Nick smirked. "I suggest you never play poker with me. I'm a great bluffer."

"How far?" Nick asked, as quietly as possible, over the prearranged comm channel that allowed him to communicate with the rebel soldiers, Bones, and Siren for the duration of the mission.

"Less than a thousand meters. We should be on it in three minutes."

"Everyone, ready. Regardless of what Dr. Oilil said, Poskin will have bodyguards," said Nick.

The building came into view as they came around a bend in a well-lit cavern ahead. Nick held up a gloved hand and the band of soldiers came to a halt.

The steel and glass building appeared deserted, with no lights visible from inside. The plaza around the structure was devoid of life. No movement or sound came from the direction of the complex.

It was quiet. Too quiet.

Nick signaled they should move slowly forward. Keeping low, they moved into the plaza, rifles at the ready. The soldiers moved to cover their flanks while Nick, Siren, and Bones went up the middle directly toward the structure. Seeing no signs of anyone, Nick moved to the twin glass doors at the entrance into the darkened building. Nick stopped and peered through the glass into the shadowy lobby.

A flash of movement caught his eye, but nothing he could discern.

111

He peered into the inky black beyond the shadows, trying to determine if he could see anyone inside. They could use the suit lamps but the shaded glass would no doubt reflect the light back at them.

We'll have to be inside to use the suit lamps.

"Bones and Siren, come with me. We're going inside. The rest of you stay out here and guard the perimeter. Understood?" A chorus of grunts and acknowledgements came over the comm as the rebel soldiers fanned out.

"Won't it be risky, boss?" asked Bones as they approached the entry doors.

Nick smiled to himself, then said, "You're probably right, Bones."

"Good," said the big man. Nick chuckled softly under his breath.

After turning on her suit lamps, Siren led the way through the doors into the lobby. Nick and Bones quickly followed and they formed a half circle to cover the largest field of fire possible in case shooting started. But the lobby was quiet, with no movement in the stuffy, stale air that smelled of age and mold. It was warm as if the air circulation system common on most Alliance worlds had been turned off.

Without lowering his rifle,

Nick turned on the beam from one of his lamps and illuminated a control panel recessed into one of the walls on either side of the lift shaft in the middle of the barren lobby. There were no decorations or furniture adorning the empty room, so every footstep echoed in the still air. There were no obvious threats present.

Nick strode up to study the panel and saw there were six sliding buttons, none of which were labeled. He slung his rifle over his back.

"Siren, take a look at this," he said.

She moved to stand beside him. Lifting the hand scanner, she scanned the panel. She made a derisive noise. "No power," she said simply.

Nick froze when he heard a muffled voice coming from the direction of the bank of lifts behind the walls. He moved around the wall nearest him and cast his suit lamps into the space. He froze when the beams of white light showed a human-shaped figure he recognized, lying on the floor. It was Lal. His arms and legs were bound and a gag had been stuffed into his mouth.

The alien's eyes were wide and angry and when the light hit him, he struggled against his bonds. His muffled words became frantic as he squirmed.

"Hello, Sub-Protector Lal," Nick said softly.

17

Milhath Continent, Sector 77, Mine shaft 47776
Brimstone V
4146.12.23 Galactic

SIREN MOVED TO untie Lal, who sucked air into his lungs after the gag was removed. "Thank you," he gasped as she managed to untie the last of the restraints from his legs.

"How long have you been here?" asked Nick.

Lal shook his head and winced. "I'm not sure. The last thing I recall before waking up here was the sound of footsteps coming up behind me in my office and then nothing. The next thing I heard was your voices."

Siren checked the back of Lal's head and nodded her confirmation that he had indeed been struck on the back of the head. But why leave him here, bound and gagged?

"What is this complex?" Nick asked.

Lal's hand moved to the back of his head and he winced as his fingers brushed the spot where he'd been hit. "It's a local government building I use as my regional headquarters whenever I'm in the Milhath District. It's an administrative only district. In fact, this entire community is a government and scientific research complex. It has no military or strategic importance if that's what you're thinking."

Nick's lips formed a wry smile. "Excuse me for saying so, Sub-Protector Lal, I assume *you* have some strategic value?"

Lal nodded slowly as color drained form his features. It had dawned on him that he could have been assassinated, which was exactly what Nick was thinking. The problem was, he hadn't been killed, only restrained. This meant he was bait. Bait to capture something or someone.

Suddenly the overhead light banks flashed on and Nick was forced to shield his eyes. A plethora of heavy footsteps echoed from both ends of the corridor, separating the banks of lifts. "Don't move," said a deep voice.

The smell of machine oil filled Nick's mouth and nose. "Who are you after?" asked Nick.

His eyes adjusted to the lights and he blinked to clear his vision.

A tall alien male came into focus. Since he didn't wear a helmet with a shaded visor, Nick could see he was human. His massive, muscular frame was covered head-to-toe in purple battle armor. In his gloved right hand, he held a large blaster pistol Nick recognized as the newest model carried by Alliance navy shock troops.

Gears had briefed him during the trip to Brimstone V about the newest blaster model's capabilities. The only important fact at this moment, since this one was aimed at his chest, was the gun had seven settings ranging from a mild stun to full disintegration. He had no idea what setting the weapon had been set to since he had no inkling of the man's intention. At least not yet.

"So," said Nick not bothering to hide the sarcasm from his tone. "The navy has arrived. Or should I say the cavalry?" He arched an eyebrow at the man.

The man smirked and his eyes reflected his amusement. "My name is Colonel Achmed. As you say, Captain Justice, we are with the AN. Our orders are to rescue you and your squad."

Nick chuckled. "Who said we needing rescuing, Colonel?"

"Chairman Whizzar," Achmed said matter of factly.

116

"And who, exactly, from?"

"The civil war on this planet is heating up and we are to evacuate you and your people immediately. We have secured Alfonso Ripe and we retrieved Musty Hobbs and your vessel from the moon orbiting Brimstone III." He paused as his gray eyes flitted to Siren, then back to him. "This woman is not Sirenna Albright."

Nick nodded. "Yes, I know. She's an artificial."

"Nick!" protested Siren's double. "How can you say that? You've known me for over twenty years."

Nick looked at the pseudo Siren. "No, I'm sorry, but you are a spy for Poskin. You have been leading us astray this whole time." He paused to look at Colonel Achmed. "Colonel, you should deploy your troops outside the building, we are about to be attacked by Poskin's soldiers. This is a trap."

Achmed signaled all except two of his troopers to exit the building and spoke in low tones into his comm to alert however many troopers they had deployed in the area surrounding the complex. If Nick knew the AN, they had deployed far more shock troops than they actually needed. Overkill wasn't in their dictionary.

Nick stepped toward Lal.

"Poskin wants to kill us and you to hide the fact they have no idea where the energy field is, and was hoping we would lead them to it. That's what this has been all about from the beginning."

Lal frowned. "But we don't have it. Poskin has it…" His voice trailed off and his eyes flared. "Neither of us has it," he whispered.

Suddenly the whine of blaster fire came from outside the building. "The attack has begun," Nick said glumly. A lot of innocent people were about to die for a technology that the opposing sides thought the other possessed.

18

Milhath Continent, Sector 77, Mine shaft 47776
Brimstone V
4146.12.23 Galactic

"COLONEL," NICK SAID, turning to face the dusky-skinned naval officer. "I imagine your orders include securing the energy field?"

The Colonel nodded.

"The readings indicating that it was here were faked. Someone did all this to capture the energy field that was stolen by these aliens. But it isn't here anymore." His eyes narrowed. "And I have no idea where it is."

The sounds of blaster fire dwindled until there was only silence. Achmed spoke into his comm. "Is the area secure?" Nick heard a muffled reply that he couldn't quite make out. Achmed looked at Nick. "The attackers who have not been neutralized have retreated."

Neutralized always sounds so civilized, thought Nick.

The reality was they had been killed, and knowing the shock troopers' reputation, enemy wounded had also been *neutralized*.

"When are we leaving?" Nick asked the colonel.

"Ten minutes until transport range, sir," came the reply from one of the armed troopers behind Colonel Achmed.

"Your materializer is capable of reaching this far underground?" asked Nick, surprised such technology existed. Not even Gears knew of such a powerful transport device. The Alliance Navy apparently had all sorts of secrets they didn't openly share.

Ignoring Nick's question, Achmed instructed Nick, Bones, and his remaining troopers to meet him outside. When the artificial copy of Siren moved to follow them, Achmed told her to stay behind.

Nick walked back to question Achmed. "Colonel, why isn't she coming with us?"

The colonel's eyes were cool and unemotional. "She is the enemy. She was part of the setup for the ambush." He grunted. "I assure you if this one had a chance, she would kill you and your squad."

"Are you going to liquidate her?" asked Nick.

"We call it neutralize, but yes, she will be killed. We don't take prisoners." His hands moved to the blaster in his holster.

"But Blaster Squad does take prisoners," said Nick, determination evident in his tone. Out of the corner of his eyes, Nick detected movement. No doubt one of Achmed's troopers had moved to his flank in case he needed to intervene in support of his commander.

"So, what do you intend to do with her?"

Nick offered the AN officer a sly smile. "I have plans for her. All I ask is you transport her to my ship and leave the rest to us."

Achmed's black eyes were curious. Nick watched the colonel's hand drop away from the butt of his blaster pistol. "Okay, Captain Justice. I'm willing to accede to your request. We are under orders from the Chairman to cooperate with you." A slow grin came across his features. "Even if your request is contrary to our standing policies."

Nick's eyes narrowed. "What is going to happen to Brimstone V?"

Achmed's mouth formed a grim, humorless smile. "We'll destroy the planet, of course. We must end the bounty hunter threat to the galaxy. They have gone too far by kidnapping Alliance citizens, thereby threatening the peace."

Nick knew there was no bargaining chip he could use to stop Achmed from carrying out his orders unless… "If I discover the location of the energy field, would that change things?"

Achmed arched an eyebrow, obviously intrigued. "Yes, it might."

Nick turned toward Siren. Placing his hands on her arms near her shoulders, he looked hard into her fearful eyes. "I know you've been told not to reveal the location of the energy field. But I can guarantee your safety if you tell us where it was taken."

Artificial Siren's features became ashen and she swallowed hard, perspiration dotted her forehead. "They'll kill me," she whispered. She didn't mean Poskin or Lal, so someone else was behind these events. There were players off the board pulling the strings and it made a knot of anger form in the pit of Nick's stomach.

Nick shook his head. "You're going to die at the hands of the Alliance Navy, either now or when they vaporize the planet. So unless you tell us what we want to know, my squad and I are your only hope for survival."

Her watery gaze pleaded with him. "Will you take me with you?"

Nick nodded. "Yes. You have my word." Nick's heart beat faster. He had the sinking feeling time for talk was running short. *I better convince her I will help her escape soon, or billions of innocent beings across the galaxy will be die.*

Her eyes steadied and her jawline became taut. "Okay," she said firmly. "The energy field was taken by my master to Brimstone III until it could be retrieved."

Achmed spoke rapidly into his comm. "Sensors report an alien vessel has materialized in orbit around Brimstone III. There are indications they have activated their materializer." He looked at Nick. "We're too late."

Nick's grip tightened around pseudo Sirens arms but she didn't flinch and her eyes remained passive. Nick stepped back, pulled his blaster, and fired.

The duplicate of Siren screamed in agony as the beam of superheated energy enveloped her. The piercing screams ended when the ruined, unrecognizable corpse that until seconds ago resembled Sirenna Albright finally collapsed to the floor. The room now stank of a stomach churning mix of charred, smoking bits of flesh clinging to blackened bones.

"Why did you do that?" asked Bones, sounding horrified.

Nick holstered his weapon. He knew he'd done the right thing. "It wasn't Siren," he said between gritted teeth. "*It* was a device designed to trick us." He glared at Bones. "She would have killed us given the opportunity." Doubt was in Bones eyes. Nick wanted to scream at him but managed to keep his voice level as he said, "Didn't you hear Colonel Achmed?"

Bones nodded, his eyes shifting to the remains of the doppelganger.

"But you promised…" Bones said his voice trailing off.

"Did I?" Nick said, his tone hard. "Let's get out of here."

Nick extended his arm. "After you, Colonel."

19

GEARS HAD SET the flight controls on automatic for the last several days. Bones, Gears, and the Kid were seated across the galley table from Nick and Siren. They each had a mug of hot tea in front of them but so far no one had taken even a sip.

Everyone was physically and emotionally exhausted after the events on Brimstone V. They all had dark circles under their eyes, reminders of their lack of sleep and their loss of appetite. Gears hadn't even asked for a glazed donut in over two weeks. This mission would stick with them all for many years to come.

This Siren was the real thing. She had been liberated by Navy shock troops an hour before they intercepted Nick and Bones. The troopers had killed several dozen civilians during her rescue. Of course, it wasn't a rescue at all.

Blaster Squad #3 Planet of Doom

She and her sister Sonara had been working together to disrupt the civil war, trying to spark peace talks. The real Lal convinced Siren to help him end the destructive war that had consumed nearly all their planetary resources. The people were starving and there was an increase in disappearances and suggestions of atrocities on both sides.

The Alliance Navy had bombarded the planet from orbit until the planetary crust was ruptured and the planet broke apart. Millions of people died. Any Brimstone ships that tried to stop the AN battle fleet from bombarding the planet were atomized before they came within weapons range by the Navy picket ships, comprised of patrol class warships that guarded the battle fleet against attack.

Nick pleaded with Colonel Achmed for a chance to recover the energy field taken by the mystery vessel that had appeared and disappeared without a trace. But this fell on deaf ears. Achmed followed his orders to the letter now that the recovery of the energy field was impossible.

Gears had been unable to track the mystery vessel after it left Brimstone III with the energy field.

Siren's sister Sonara managed to escape aboard her private FTL ship before the navy attacked.

Her ship was small, and faster at sublight speeds than the *Hunter*. Gears tracked it until it left the system, then lost it when it jumped to FTL.

"I have to ask," said Siren sullenly.

"What?" said Nick softly.

"Why did you kill my doppelganger after you promised to save her from Achmed?"

Nick grunted. "I knew if I didn't kill her, Achmed would torture her, then kill her slowly even after she revealed the location of the enemy vessel. He's a sadistic monster who enjoys killing."

Gears looked up from his steaming mug of tea. "How would she know the position of that vessel when we can't track it and apparently neither can the navy?"

"Because, my dear friends, she placed a tracking device on that ship and downloaded the tracking information into my hand scanner," said Nick.

"What?" Bones cried. "Who are they?"

Nick shook his head. "I don't know yet. But once we reach Earth, I'm going to ask Asia to help us find this master the artificial Siren mentioned. I suspect my mentor and oldest friend knows more than she let on the last time we talked."

Collective nods around the table brought a smile to Nick's lips.

It quickly faded when he recalled the death of Siren's duplicate. He'd had no choice. He'd saved her as he promised, but in the way she hadn't expected.

The real Siren told him the bounty hunter that attacked her over twenty years ago hadn't been sent to kill her. The plan was to kidnap her and hold her for ransom, something bounty hunters were especially adept at. But Lal's mate had failed to realize Siren's counter attack would be so effective.

Lal accepted Siren's explanation for what happened. He realized she was defending herself and that his mate made the wrong decision to draw her weapon when she did without explaining her actions first.

The terms of the contract provided that after the bounty hunters received their cut of the ransom the remainder was to be paid to a person referred to as the Master through an intermediary. Siren said Lal knew this because he had researched the intermediary's background and discovered the person known as the Master was behind the plot, but not where they could find him or her.

Another needless death, thought Nick somberly. Someday he would find this master and make him or her pay a terrible price for these deaths.

Russ Crossley

* * *

Blaster Squad will return in their next exciting
adventure, *Raiders of Cloud City*,
coming soon from 53rd Street Publishing.

About the Author

INTERNATIONAL SELLING AUTHOR, Russ Crossley, writes science fiction and fantasy, and mystery/suspense as well as their various subgenres.

His latest science fiction satire set in the far future, Revenge of the Lushites, is a sequel to Attack of the Lushites released in 2011. The latest title in the series was released in the fall of 2013. Both titles are available in e-book and trade paperback.

He has sold several short stories that have appeared in anthologies from various publishers including; WMG Publishing, Pocket Books, 53rd Street Publishing, and St. Martins Press.

He is a member of SF Canada and is past president of the Greater Vancouver Chapter of Romance Writers of America. He is also an alumni of the Oregon Coast Professional Fiction Writers Master Class taught by award winning author/editors, Kristine Katherine Rusch and Dean Wesley Smith.

Feel free to contact him on Facebook, Twitter, or his website http//:www.russcrossley.com. He loves to hear from readers.

Other titles by Russ Crossley you may enjoy
Razor and Edge Mysteries
The Kidnapping of Billy Buttons
String of Pearls
Death by Clown
Beggin' For Murder
Ragged Ice
The Grand Central Mystery
A Strange Case of Undead Murder

Jazz Stiletto Mysteries
A Day Without Sunshine
Skullduggery
Instrument of justice (first published in Over My
Dead Body online mystery magazine)

The Amanda Dark paranormal mysteries
Hook Island
Grind Manor
Moonrise Diner
A Father's Daughter

The Trudy Wilson Mystery Novel Series
Bad Loyalty
Shear Murder
Buzzcut - coming soon

Blaster Squad
#1 Terror on the Moon
#2 Sea of Death
#3 Planet of Doom
#4 Raiders of Cloud City (coming soon)

Other Novels

Attack of the Lushites
Revenge of the Lushites
My Zombie Prince
Antique Virgin
The Fire In Their Hearts
with R.S. Meger (from Champagne Books)
Zomopolis
The Last Serial Killer

Short Stories
Countdown
Shoeless Moe
Round Up At The Burger Bar:
The Story of Trixie Pug, Parts 1, 2, 3, 4, 5, 6, 7, 8, 9
Five Minutes
Blossom Queen, Barbarian
The Secret
The Family Line
End of the Flies
Death by Magic
The Penguin Sleeps With The Fishes
Only The Worthy
Hero For A Day
End of Empire
Strange Bedfellows
Big Business
A Perfect Crime
The Wise Guy and The Pirates
In Search of the Perfect Cup

T.I.N. Men
The Legend of G and the Dragonettes
The Incredible Mr. Fix-It
Lock Stock and Barrel
Divided Loyalties
Cave of Wonders
A Family Empire
Until We Meet Again
Dragon Rising
Solitary Man
The Keel Mountain Conspiracy
Angel on My Shoulder
Heroes of Old
The Great Bicycle Race
Tikka's Big Day
"My Partner the Zombie" —
Hungry For Your Love Anthology
(St. Martin's Press)
Big Hairy Deal
One Red Shoe
A Bad Day in Lunden Texas
Bloody Betty, Queen of the Pirates
Mirror Image
Dangerous Waters
Cape Disappointment
Boomerang
The Watcher of Wayburn Street
The Apprentice
Drip!
A Beautiful Friendship and The Parrot of Doom
Robine's Diary
The Christmas Club

Loose Ends
Splatter Pattern
It Takes Two
Lexicon
Replacement Parts
Sidekicks
Lost Stories
Time and Space
Survivors
Neighborhood Watch
Unnatural Immortal
Rum Runner's Lounge
It's A Small Galaxy
A Shattered Man
Betrayed
Replacement Parts
Clubhouse Heroes
Sounds That Angels Make
Muggins Rules – originally published in Fiction River
Volume 12, Risk Takers

Anthologies
Tales of Urban Fantasy
Five Tales of Bizarre Detectives
Tales of Mystery and Suspense
Tales of Weird Fantasy
Tales of Twisted Crime
Tales of The Unexpected
Tales From Space
10 by Russ Crossley
Round Up At The Burger Bar: The Story of Trixie
Pug,

Parts 1- 5 The Beginning
Worlds of Science Fiction and Fantasy
More Tales of Mystery and Suspense
Justice Served
Love Stories
Ladies of the Jolly Roger with Rita Schulz
The Adventures of Razor and Edge:
Five Tales From The Quirky Detective Team
An Unexpected Journey
On Edge
Thrilling Adventures
Total War
Courageous

Non-Fiction
The Writers Tools - The Synopsis

Also available from 53rd Street Publishing
http://www.53rdstreetpublishing.com

In the 42nd century alien pirates steal a deadly virus
threatening to wipe out billions of lives. A team of
highly trained mercenaries known as Blaster Squad
springs into action to stop the pirates deadly plot and
save the galaxy from certain doom.

Blaze across the galaxy with Blaster Squad a new
brand of mercenaries who are willing to break all the
rules to win.

Nick Justice (aka Justice)

The charismatic leader of the squad is an expert with all weapons; knives, blaster rifles and pistols, and has a double black belt in Karate.
Nick has his own definition of right and wrong regardless of who disagrees that often leads to trouble.

Sirenna Albright (aka Siren)

She is the second in command. Siren is an expert in all forms of martial arts, and a deadly shot with a blaster pistol and rifle.

Her beauty and mysterious past make her a riddle within an enigma and a valuable member of the squad.

Rocky Bones (aka Bones)

Born on the Mars colony Bones has enhanced strength due to the bones in his arms and legs being replaced with high tech composite metals.

A giant of a man skilled with all forms of weaponry who never shies away from certain death.

Musty Hobbs (aka Gears)

Half human-half half Cygnus IV alien hybrid. He's a

scientific genius who can defeat any security system, can pilot any spacecraft, and has an eidetic memory. An expert with blasters and has enhanced vision due to ocular implants he is a deadly adversary when cornered.

Alfonso Ripe (aka The Kid)
The newest recruit to the squad he is skilled with explosives and blasters. He and Gears constantly butt heads and the tech genius doesn't trust him.

Nick isn't convinced he's a good fit for the squad, but for now they need his skills.

Look for this title in ebook and print editions at your favorite online retailer or ask for it at our local bookstore.